Truth

C. L. Poehlmann

This book is dedicated to you. As you read this book, may your heart and mind be stretched, and may a passion to live out your destiny be ignited in you. With God all things are possible.

ACKNOWLEDGMENTS

To the amazing people God has put in my life to help with this writing journey—Mari Nelle, Kenzie, Gayle, Anna, Chris, Jessica and Gary—thank you for your generosity, help, support, and love. I am very blessed to have you in my life.

To my Mom and Dad—thank you for being the best parents. You truly instilled in me that with God all things are possible. They really are.

To my amazing friends and family who give me incredible support and encouraged me to press on—Phil, Jeff, Elaine, Carol, Joanna, Lorea, Kimberly, Steph, Beth, Ben, Toby, Todd, Ron, Kris, Meg, and last, but certainly not least, Tom—you guys rock.

NOTE FROM THE AUTHOR

The idea for this story first came to me ten years before I actually wrote a single word of this novel. It took me those ten years to find the courage to write the story, and another five years to publish it, all the while being fully dependent upon God's love and the support of family and friends to press forward. It was my heart's desire to see a book about a modern day character that anyone could relate to, set on planet Earth, and containing the power of God that ultimately brought this book to fruition.

I do not hold a degree related to writing, nor was it my life's long dream to be a writer, but as I began to write this story, a hidden talent and passion began to emerge. It was as if I was watching a movie in my mind, and I simply wrote what I saw. The majority of the novel was written in three weeks, and it took me another three months to join it all together. With the help of family, the next five years were spent editing.

During that time, the publishing industry went through a major change with the rise of eBooks and affordable self-publishing companies. There were times I doubted that I would find a way to get it published, but when a need arose, there was a person in my life that could fill that need. It has been quite an adventure. If you enjoyed this novel, please join me, C. L. Poehlmann, on Facebook or www.clpoehlmann.com and keep up-to-date on the progress of the sequels to *Truth*.

Contents

Prologue

Chapter 1. Shades of Blue   1

Chapter 2. To Tell the Truth   13

Chapter 3. Episodes   29

Chapter 4. Then Death   41

Chapter 5. Pumpkin Fest   55

Chapter 6. My Thoughts; Your Thoughts   77

Chapter 7. Friend or Foe   91

Chapter 8. The Gathering   101

Chapter 9. The Child   115

Chapter 10. Space-Time Continuum   131

Chapter 11. The Figure   141

Chapter 12. A Marriage Proposal   151

Chapter 13. The Engagement   161

Chapter 14. History of a Town   175

Chapter 15. Bolt from the Blue   187

Epilogue   215

Prologue

I had recently come to accept that anything was possible with God through His amazing power and abilities, which was great and could be very helpful in situations such as this one, but unfortunately I also believed that we all die at some point. My friend died once, and even though he was brought back from the dead, he told me that he still remembered the pain of his violent death.

My surroundings and situation were becoming all too real. The cold damp floor slowly leached the heat from my body, the restraints that held my wrists behind my back began to cut my skin, and mentally I struggled with the prospects of my future. What would be the miracle that would allow me to escape? Or would I be killed and somehow brought back from the dead? Could I bear to live with the memories of my own tragic death for the rest of my earthly life? Dan had fervently expressed his concern for me, and his desire to keep me from a fate such as that. Did he somehow know what would happen?

My mind drifted to a more disturbing thought: *what if I die, but I'm not brought back to life?*

1

Shades of Blue

"Ruthy, if you don't get your rear in gear we're gonna be late!"

I was standing on our deck looking out over the Pacific Ocean, possibly for the last time, trying to capture the landscape in my memory when my dad rudely interrupted me.

"Okay, Dad! I'll be right there."

We had moved to California three months after the sale of our farm in Nebraska had been finalized. I was not sad to leave California, but there was something calming about the water that I would miss. And that day, for some reason, the ocean was extraordinarily beautiful–a pristine aqua–as if it was wishing me farewell. I love the ocean. The ocean is graceful, unrelenting, powerful, and inviting–all the things that I am not. I am awkward, shy, weak, and most of all, unlovable–I am a freak.

I bent down and picked up my bag, took one more look at the ocean, then headed to the moving truck where I would be entombed for the next four days with my entire family–which now consisted of just me and my dad.

Dad is only forty-five years old, but the past year had aged him to the point that he looked closer to fifty-five. He always wore sunscreen and long sleeves, but even with all that, the California sun had given him an unfamiliar dark tan. Over the past three months he had darkened to a warm shade of brown, similar to the color of twelve ounces of 2% milk and three tablespoons of chocolate syrup.

I had gotten halfway to the truck when I heard Mrs. Arnold, our next-door neighbor, calling out. "Eli. Ruth. Wait!" I started walking faster, pretending that I had not heard her. She had been my neighbor for three months, but I really did not know her that well, and I tend to fidget and stutter around strangers. I managed to slide in the passenger seat just as Mrs. Arnold reached the truck.

"Eli, I've made you and Ruthy some sandwiches and crispy rice bars for your trip." She handed Dad a small, white, plastic grocery bag.

"Thanks, Mrs. Arnold. That's kind of you."

Unfortunately, I had not escaped Mrs. Arnold's attention. She stuck her head in the driver's side door and said, "Honey, you don't have to go."

What could I say to that dear old woman? I did not want to stay. I never wanted to move to California in the first place. I started to perspire as the rhythm of my heartbeat pounded in my head. Mrs. Arnold turned to my dad for an answer.

"My daughter's offer still stands. Phyllis assures me she has a place for Ruth at her private school, and they even have a scholarship that would pay for her tuition."

"That is sweet of you, but with the controversy surrounding Ruthy's school and that whole tragedy, I think it's best we go." Dad handed me the white bag and his jacket. I was curious, so I took a peak into the bag, but I was disappointed to find pimento cheese and liver loaf sandwiches–Dad could eat those.

"Are you sure you have to leave?"

Dad peeked over at me, and I shot him a look of exasperation. Mrs. Arnold had been trying to set Dad and Phyllis up from the moment we moved in next door.

"Thanks again, Mrs. Arnold, but we really must leave–time's a tickin'."

Dad was determined to reach Gilpinton, Missouri by Tuesday evening, so bright and early Friday morning at a quarter till seven (a time that I had protested), we ventured out across the country.

I am *not* a morning person!

Friday was perfect–pleasant and sunny–the temperature a magnificent seventy-one degrees. After much contemplation on the matter, I had come to the conclusion that seventy-one degrees Fahrenheit was the perfect temperature. A jacket is not required, yet I can tolerate wearing blue jeans and a long sleeve shirt. Friday, a perfect day, and I am stuck in a truck.

Dad climbed in the truck and started the engine. "Buckle up, honey. So what did Mrs. Arnold send with us?"

"Your favorite, pimento cheese and liver loaf sandwiches."

"She is a sweet old lady–I'll give her that, but she was always trying to get into our business."

I leaned my head against my side window as we drove away. I watched the apartment shrink in the mirror until we turned the corner and then it was gone.

"Ruthy? Ruthy, roll down the window if you're getting sick. I don't want to spend the next five hundred miles smelling like vomit."

"I'm fine, Dad." I was not aggravated with him. His was a normal response of someone who had spent any length of time around me. My body openly expressed my heart in such a way that allowed everyone to witness my joy, pain, frustration, and sorrow. Sometimes my ears turned red when I was embarrassed or upset, I vomited when I was nervous, and I fainted when my emotions overwhelmed me. I fainted a lot.

The trip went remarkably well with no incident. I loaded my iPod with a bunch of new songs and a few movies. I stayed fairly entertained. There was only a couple times when the trip became miserable. It is amazing how tired you get simply sitting for hours.

I would have to admit that I had been looking forward to a cross-country trip. The view would certainly not be boring, and even though I would miss the ocean, a change of scenery could be a useful distraction. We started our trip with a view of the ocean, then we traveled over mountains, across the plains, and finally we ended up at the foothills of the Ozark Mountains. It was early October, and the closer we got to Missouri the more beautiful the fall foliage.

Gilpinton was a rather small town with only about 1,500 people. Compared to the city where I lived in California, it was no more than a speck on a map. But I grew up near Valentine, Nebraska, out in the country, so to me any collection of homes closer than a quarter of a mile was considered a metropolis. I had been to Gilpinton over a dozen times in my life–my aunt and uncle on my dad's side live there. They have one son, Rawden Jefferson Davis the third–said with that low tone that makes it sound like a dignified name. But everyone calls him Rawdy. I started calling him Rawdy when I was five years old, and it has stuck ever since– which I might add, has always ticked off my Aunt Marge. I know it might sound twisted, but I found a strange sense of accomplishment in renaming him.

The first night we stayed in a small motel just off the road in the middle of nowhere. I was exhausted. I quickly prepared for bed and was out almost instantly.

"Jacob, you're alright!" I exclaimed.

"Ruthy, you weren't supposed to be here. Not today."

"Jacob, it's so good to see you!"

Jacob and I were standing in the hallway. He was dressed in jeans and a tee-shirt, but I still had on my nightgown.

"What are you doing here, Jacob?"

"This is all your fault, Ruthy."

"No, Jacob, don't say that. What've I done?"

"You know what you did, and it's all your fault."

"No, Jacob, please! Please don't do this!" I started crying and he began to run down the hall.

"Come back. Please don't leave! Come back, Jacob!" I ran after him, but I could not keep up. When I got to the corner, Mr. Grandfield stepped in front of me asking, "Where do you think you're going? Remember, no running in the halls."

"Where did Jacob go?" I was trying to look over Mr. Grandfield's shoulder, but I did not see Jacob anywhere. He was gone.

"It's your fault, Ruthy. He's gone because of you."

"No! I'm sorry. I'm so sorry!"

"It's your fault and you can't bring him back. He's gone forever and it's all your fault."

Jacob walked around the corner. I tried to reach out to him, but he pushed my hands away. Mr. Grandfield and Jacob both began walking toward me. Then in unison they started saying, "It's all your fault, Ruthy. It's all your fault."

"No. Stop saying that. Please!"

"You know it's your fault, and now it's too late."

"No!" I screamed.

"Ruthy! Ruthy, honey, wake-up!" Dad was pleading with me. Reality slowly set in, and I knew it had all been a dream. Some might even have called it a nightmare, but I could not call it that. No. I had just seen Jacob—I could never call that a nightmare.

We arrived in Gilpinton right on track with Dad's schedule and before a coming storm. Dad had perfectly packed the moving truck in order of importance. When we opened the back door of the truck, our bedroom furnishings were first, then the living room stuff. My dad could not be without his jumbo, flat screen, high definition, 3D TV. Mom never let him have a television, so as soon as they were divorced, Dad went out and bought his dream TV. After the living room stuff was the kitchen supplies, and finally the garage odds and ends. You could always count on my dad to have everything in order, but the past year I had learned that not even he could fix everything.

To my delight, my aunt and uncle came over with a couple of Uncle Rick's buddies and Rawdy's friend, Sarah. We unpacked the truck in record time–just under two hours. It was midnight when my head hit my pillow.

I was comfortably settled into my oh-so-wonderful bed when I noticed that my iPod was missing. I remembered having it in the cab of the truck when we passed Kingdom City. I remembered because my favorite love song was playing when we passed a truck with the most gorgeous guy I had ever seen. It was one of those moments when you wonder if there was some form of divine intervention at work.

I put on my flip flops and ran down the stairs. The rain had temporarily slowed to a steady drizzle. I had no idea where an umbrella was, or even where one should be, so I decided to make a run for it. I got to the truck door, grabbed the handle and tried to open it, but of course the door was locked. I am sure it was the only locked vehicle on the block, or even in the town, but Dad had grown accustomed to living in a big city and that forced me to run back to the house.

I got to the front door and heard a noise–it sounded like tin cans rattling. I was not really scared–it was not that kind of sound–but it crossed my mind that I might not be alone. I grabbed the keys and my Hot Shot from my purse—Dad bought it for me right before we moved to California; it is a farm boy thing. It gives off a short zap that hurts, but it would not do any permanent damage. It is not a Taser gun.

I returned to the truck, unlocked it, and found the iPod right where I had left it. I could easily make it back to the porch in six large steps. Sarah and I had made a game earlier in the evening of counting our steps back and forth from the truck to the house. I concluded that six large steps were the least I could take and make it to the front door, yet if I took eleven smaller steps I would be sure not to slip on the wet grass.

I heard the noise again and looked down the street. There were street lights on, but with the drizzle it was hard to see more than two houses away. I decided six steps was my fastest route to the house. One…Two…Three…

"Whoa!…Ouch!…Hey!"

"Oh! I didn't see you there!" I heard as I was knocked to the ground.

"Sorry!" was the boy's only word of apology as he ran past me–he did not even offer to help me up!

I was soaked, but thankfully my iPod was safe in my front pants pocket. If it had still been in my hand it would have been smashed to bits. I had fallen flat on my rear end with my legs straight in front of me. Both of my hands were covered in mud; I tried to enter the house and keep the door handle clean, but that was impossible.

I could not believe that guy ran right into me and then simply left. What was he doing out in the rain? He looked like he had been running from something, and obviously he had not seen me standing there until he plowed into me, which led me to believe he was looking behind him when he ran into me. I did not know anyone on our street, so it was pointless for me to rack my brain wondering who or what he was running from. Positively a waste of time to consider if he could have been sneaking out of someone's room, or sneaking out of his own house. Was he spying on someone, or was he in trouble and running away in fear of someone? That last thought sent me inside, making certain I locked the door. I tested the dead bolt to make sure it was locked, and then turned around and leaned back on the door relieved. Just then a bizarre thought consumed me. Something deep inside me made me wonder if this town was truly as typical as things appeared. Gilpinton was the epitome of small town America, but that did not mean it lacked crime. It just meant everyone knew about it as soon as it happened.

Monday morning rolled around way too early. This school started earlier than my last one, and prior to that I had been homeschooled. My mom was not fond of the public school system. Principal Andrews had told my dad, "She must be there at 7:00 sharp."

I am not a morning person!

My dad had called the school the day before we left California. He wanted to make sure he had all the paperwork needed to enroll me right away. I was a straight "A" student, and Dad did not want me falling behind due to our relocating twice in one year. I would have enough trouble fitting in with a bunch of new kids. I did not need any additional stress. Back in Nebraska, my mom had homeschooled me, and we lived on a farm that was out in the middle of nowhere. Mom always made sure I had kids to play with, but I was not a girly girl, and I was taller and could run faster than most of the boys my age. All of that amounted to me not having many friends, but it left plenty of time for my studies. Thankfully, this school used the same curriculum as the last one and started two weeks later in the fall. And even though I would miss several days of school due to travel, I was still ahead in my studies by at least a week which made the first week an easier transition.

By the time I got my schedule and was shown around the campus (which took all of twenty minutes), my first class was half over. I did not mind. I hate being the center of attention, and because the class was almost over, Mr. Caldwell just pointed to the empty seat and went on with his lecture. Mr. Caldwell was a good teacher, but he had bad breath and a very unusual habit which involved putting Vaseline up his nose. I guess I might not think it was that unusual if he had not done it in front of the *entire* class. That was a teacher just asking to be harassed.

Thankfully, this school was small enough for the entire high school student body to eat lunch at the same time, allowing me to sit by Rawdy and his friend, Sarah. I hate to eat alone. All morning long I had been given the only empty seat in each of my classes. I liked not having to choose who I sat by. Everyone was a stranger to me anyway. All in all, the first part of the day went fairly well. I had not fainted once.

It was not until lunch that I had the opportunity to look at everyone's face and find my tackler from last night. I scanned the crowd, methodically examining each table, one by one. I had almost given up hope of finding him when I looked up and down Rawdy's table. There he was, sitting on the other side of Rawdy. Rawdy noticed me staring at my tackler and introduced us.

"Mike, this is my cousin, Ruthy."

Mike said, "Oh yeah, you're that girl."

"Yeah! You didn't even try to help me up!" I said, with a little too much anger. I even surprised myself with my bold statement.

Mike looked appalled. "Well, you see, I was in...a hurry. I'm sorry."

Coming from a jock, I figured that was the best apology I would get, yet I could tell in his eyes that he truly was sorry. He surprised me when he continued saying, "How can I make it up to you, Ruthy?"

"Don't worry about it, Mike. No harm, no foul. Right?"

"Yeah, something like that. But I really would like to apologize and try to make it up to you."

"Really, Mike, I'm fine. I just got a little wet and muddy, but nothing was broken. Just don't do it again, and we'll be fine."

My mystery was solved, or was it? I knew who had run me over, but that was not the entire mystery. Why was he running in the rain? I was afraid I would embarrass him if I pushed the issue. I decided to drop it for now, the guys had gone back to their conversation about football, and I did not feel bold enough to interrupt.

I could not stop thinking about what would cause Mike to be running in the dark while it was raining, but my thoughts were interrupted when a magnificent guy walked into the cafeteria. He was perfect. Not as tall as Rawdy, but taller than me. He stood six feet tall, give or take an inch. He had straight black hair in a trendy short style. He was a medium build, not a jock, but no one would call him frail. If I had to guess, I would say he was into rock climbing. He was dressed very classy with blue jeans and a white button down shirt. He had one of those chiseled faces, exposing high cheekbones and a sharp jaw line, capturing the attention of every girl, even the snobby ones.

Despite his great body and fabulous face, it was his eyes that captivated. They were the most beautiful shade of blue I had ever seen, like cobalt-blue glass. My mom would have called them "Brian Bloom eyes". Brian was some actor on a soap opera she used to watch as a teenager. I realized I had been staring at him without blinking, which caused my contacts to become cloudy. I had been having trouble with them all morning long. I started blinking repeatedly and finally resigned to an old trick a friend had taught me. I removed each contact one at a time, putting each into my mouth, using my tongue and spit to scrub them. I put back the right contact and then followed the same process with the left. When I had perfectly positioned the left one, I looked at him again, and to my surprise...he was staring back at me! Did he see me do that? Yes, he must have because he chuckled. Oh my, I could hardly...breathe. How embarrassing!

2

To Tell the Truth

As I watched him glide across the room, my heart began to race. He was headed straight for my table–staring directly at me! Half-way across the room he smiled, and I involuntarily smiled back. *"Breathe,"* I kept telling myself, *"Breathe,"* until finally he was standing directly across the table from me.

"Breathe." I am such a *freak!*

He pulled back a chair and said, "Is this seat taken, Sarah?"

I could feel the heat of embarrassment on my ears. Oh, so Sarah was the reason he had come to my table. She had been one of Rawdy's closest friends for as long as I could remember. Maybe he had been smiling and looking into Sarah's eyes instead of mine. I took a peek to see if she was staring into his gorgeous blue eyes, but I was utterly surprised to find her eyes fixed on a book she was holding in her lap. She had only slightly responded to his question with a nippy reply of, "No."

How could she not be mesmerized by his amazing eyes? I instinctively glanced back at his face and noticed that he was definitely not looking at Sarah. *"Breathe."* How could a simple, involuntary action, such as breathing be such an impossible task?

As he opened his milk he said, "Aren't you going to introduce me to your friend, Sarah?" Once again she replied with a short, "No." *Can she not see how beautiful he is, how beautiful his eyes are? What is wrong with her?*

He slipped his hand across the table for me to shake and said, "Well then, let me introduce myself. I'm Daniel, and you are?"

"I'm Ruth, but my family and friends call me Ruthy."

"Well, it's nice to meet you, Ruth."

"You–you–you can call me Ruthy. That's Ruthy with a 'y', not 'ie'. It's just a nickname, but I've never liked the look of it when it's spelled with an 'ie'. What do you think?" I heard the words spewing out of my mouth before I even had time to process them. He must think I am an idiot! He obviously did not consider us to be friends at that point, so why would he have called me Ruthy? And why would he care how I spelled my *name?*

He just chuckled and said, "Ok...Ruthy. You can call me Dan."

After a short awkward silence, Dan said, "So, how's your day going?"

"Pretty good."

"Well, that's good. I guess you're Rawdy's cousin?"

"Yeah, we're first cousins. Our parents are twins. They like to call each other womb-mates." He lightly laughed, but I am sure he did not care about that either, and I do not know why I said it.

"I'm sorry. I don't know why I told you all that. I tend to get nervous around strangers."

I did not think Sarah had been listening to our conversation, but she chimed in saying, "That's an understatement." I glared back at her, but Dan was the only one watching me.

"Don't worry about it. But maybe I should be taking advantage of this opportunity. You might give away some of your secrets."

I sat straight up in my chair and blurted out, "No way!"

Dan reached his hand across the table and lightly grabbed my forearm. "I'm sorry. I was just joking around."

Rawdy's head snapped around and said, "Dude, get your hands off of her."

Sarah looked up from her book and said, "Rawdy, calm down. Ruthy misunderstood what Dan was saying."

Dan quickly removed his hand from my arm while I turned toward Rawdy. "Please, Rawdy. This is my fault." I leaned close enough that I could whisper in his ear and said, "I'm nervous. He touched me, and he's so cute..."

Before I could finish my statement, he pulled away and said, "You think he's cute? Come on, guys, let's get out of here. I'm tired of watching these two flirt."

Oh my goodness. Did he really just say that? All the blood rushed out of my ears, my entire head actually, and I felt like electricity was shooting back and forth from my toes to my fingertips. I was so embarrassed! My only consolation was that Dan was not looking at me. He was staring down at his plate with an expression that could be embarrassment or irritation. I could not tell, but I assumed it was irritation. Why would he like me?

Rawdy stood up, along with most of our table–Sarah included. "Ruthy, you ready to go?"

I looked down at my plate realizing I had not taken the time to eat a single bit. "I better grab a few bites. I'll catch up to you after school. Okay?"

Rawdy looked across the table at Dan, then simply said, "Sure, I'll catch ya later."

I was not sure why Rawdy was acting that way, but I did not want to make an issue of it either, so I started eating. I did not need to give myself another reason to faint today. Usually my fainting was not caused by a lack of nutrition, but I was not about to push my luck.

Dan and I sat in silence, slowly eating, but after a few minutes we started talking again. This time I was able to keep my babbling to a minimum. Surprisingly, our conversation seemed to flow with ease, and by the end of lunch he was assuring me that he would give me assistance in any class. He was taking college prep courses and was a volunteer tutor. I could hardly believe that a guy so fit and good looking could be that smart–the total package. Through our long conversation, I found out that I had been right in assessing him as a rock climber. He offered to take me on his next trip, but I gracefully bowed out, explaining that my dad would not approve. I categorically hate heights, but was unwilling to share my neurosis with him just yet. We were both still sitting in the cafeteria when the bell rang.

"Ruthy, would you like to meet some of my friends after school? I'm not tutoring this afternoon, so we could all go for an ice cream."

I am not sure if I was more interested in getting to know him or in the chocolate, chocolate dipped cone I was envisioning. All I knew was this guy kept getting better and better, and I was not about to turn down chocolate.

As soon as the last bell rang, we were out the front door and piled into Dan's car. There were five of us in his car and four in another. I knew Sarah and Dan, but everyone else was a stranger. I could not put my finger on it, but I felt completely safe with these people. The entire group was extremely happy and friendly. All day long, most people had been commenting on my "California clothes", but not this group. No one even mentioned what I was wearing, and most of them wanted to know about my family, and about my hobbies and interests. I decided to keep my answers simple. No reason to scare these people off too soon.

When we got to the ice cream shop, one of the girls, named Haddy, was determined to stay right by my side and converse the entire time we ate.

"Oh, Ruthy, that is a beautiful necklace. Where did you get it?"

"My grandmother gave it to me." I decided not to tell her how it had belonged to a distant grandmother, and how I had to promise my grandmother that I would protect it at all cost. I thought Nana was being a little paranoid making me recite a pledge, but she did not give me a choice. She said her grandmother had given it to her and had made her promise the same thing.

"What is the little flower on it?"

"It's a blooming thistle. It's the national symbol of Scotland."

Haddy held out her hand and asked, "May I see it?"

"Sure." I slipped the long chain over my neck and handed it to her.

"It's so beautiful. Oh, and it's a locket!"

"Yeah, but it's stuck shut." She examined it a while longer and then handed it back to me.

"Very pretty. So, Ruthy, tell me about yourself."

"My dad and I moved here from California. I like to bake, but most of all I enjoy reading a good book."

Haddy said, "You must have had an amazing trip. I've never been out of the state."

"Yeah, the scenery was amazing, but it was a long trip. So you-you've really never been out of the state?"

"I never had a reason to leave. All of my family lives within a twenty-five mile radius of Gilpinton, and everything I've ever needed I can get here or on the internet."

"It must be nice to live so close to your family."

"Well, most of the time it's great, but sometimes it can be overwhelming. I have thirty-one first cousins."

"Wow, I would say so!"

"My grandparents were big supporters of adoption."

I wanted to tell her that I would trade her places, but I was not sure she could understand why I would not know where my own mother lived. Haddy was a short blonde with chocolate brown eyes. She was a sweet girl and seemed to find pleasure in anything. I overheard someone say, "Haddy is our little ray of sunshine. She's never in a bad mood."

Personally, I could not imagine that any of them were ever in a bad mood. An air of peace and complete happiness surrounded all of them. I could not remember the last time I laughed so much. My muscles were starting to hurt from the smile frozen on my face.

I do not know what caused it exactly or when it hit me. But it did. I found myself staring down at a small, wet spot on the pavement. Dan ran to my side.

"Ruthy, are you okay? Ruthy? Come on, Ruthy, answer me!"

I slowly looked up and had to wipe my eyes in order to see through the tears. "I'm alright, Dan."

"Well, you don't look alright! What is it? Did we say something? Does something hurt?" Dan was frustrated but not mad, maybe even a little scared.

"No, really I'm fine. I'm just a bit overwhelmed. It's been a long first day."

"Sure?"

"Yeah, I'm sure. Can you take me home?"

Unfortunately, before we could leave, Rawdy drove up and witnessed the event. He ran over and right away thought Dan had done something to me. Rawdy grabbed a clump of his shirt. By the look on Dan's face, I can safely assume he has chest hair.

"Rawden Jefferson, let go of him. He hasn't done anything to me."

"Then why are you crying?"

"You know . . . it's an episode."

"Again? Here? What set you off this time?" He was eyeing Dan suspiciously.

"Please, Rawdy, let him go."

He finally let go saying, "Sorry, dude."

"Ouch. I'll be fine." Dan was rubbing his chest.

"Ruthy, I'll take you home. Let's go," demanded Rawdy.

Dan was looking at me with suspicion and concern, but he was obviously not going to do or say anymore–he would never come between two family members. Rawdy grabbed a hold of my arm and tried to pull, but I refused to move.

"Ruthy, it's time to go. Get in the car." Rawdy squawked the orders at me. I looked at Dan, willing him with my pleading eyes to give me a ride.

Thankfully, Dan understood. "Would you please allow me the privilege of driving Ruthy home? And if you're willing, could you drop a few of my friends off back at the school? They rode here with us, and I don't want to leave them stranded," Dan explained, stopping momentarily between each question as he watched Rawdy's reaction. He spoke with tenderness and sincerity. No one could have refused him.

Rawdy looked at me with intense scrutiny, but I nodded my head and mouthed, "Please." He put his hand on Dan's shoulder and gave him an unmistakable look that told him that if he messed with me his sentence would be death.

Dan replied, "I'll take very good care of her. I promise you that."

Dan pointed to his car, and we started walking.

"Thanks. I'm sorry about all that. I'm not sure what's up with Rawdy."

"No problem. He cares about you. I can understand."

We were only a block away when I broke out in tears again. Without saying a word, Dan pulled over into a parking lot.

"What's going on?"

"Oh, Dan, I feel so strange!"

"Are you sick?"

I thought about it for a second. I do not feel light headed. There is no electricity shooting through my body. I could honestly say, "No, I'm *not* sick."

"Do you think it's food poisoning?"

"No! I'm not sick."

"Well, then what is it, Ruthy?"

"I think I'm really ha–happy."

Dan looked at me with confusion and said, "You're crying... because you're happy? I don't understand. Should I call your dad?"

With those words, I snapped my head up and shouted, "No!"

"Look, Ruthy, I don't want to upset you, but I don't understand what's going on, and I don't know what to do to fix this."

"I just want you to listen to me. Be quiet for a minute and let me explain, would you?"

I spoke with a little too much aggression by the look on his face, but then a smile appeared, and he settled back in his seat and said, "Ok, Ruthy, I'm all ears. If you start crying, I won't do anything. And I won't say anything until you tell me you're done."

"Thanks. I'm sure this hasn't been easy to watch."

And then it happened, just for a split second a face flashed in front of my eyes. The face of the only man I had ever loved, and it was clear that I could not explain to Dan. It was my dad's face. It was all I could do to look Dan straight in the eyes, put on a smile, and tell him "I'm really just...happy! It's been...a hard year...well, and I'm happy to be around friends again." I thought about explaining how hard it had been since my mom left, and how exhausting it was to put on a front for my dad, but I did not know him that well, and I did not know if I could trust him. And I had not lied, but I had not told him the whole truth either, and now I just gave him a lame excuse.

I could not hurt my dad again. It had only been a few days since the last time I had exposed what I was...who I was...or whatever you would call me. I do not even know the answer, so how can I explain it to Dan? Why would he ever want to spend time with me again? There has only been one word that ever even came close to describing me. And my mind was screaming it at me. *Freak. Ruthy, you're such a freak!*

I sat staring at Dan waiting for him to comment for what seemed like at least five minutes, but he was just sitting there. I finally said, "Well, aren't you going to say something?"

"Oh, so I can talk now? You're done?"

"Yes, I'm done." I know he must have thought I was an idiot, but he did not have to be sarcastic about it.

"Really? Because it seemed to me like there was something major going on. Why couldn't you just tell me this before, with the others, with Rawdy? Instead of putting my life in jeopardy."

"I guess I was embarrassed about crying. Really, Dan, I'm fine, and Rawdy is all talk." That was not a lie. I hate to cry in front of people. I was mustering all my strength, and to my surprise I was actually starting to feel better. There was something about Dan that made me feel safe–even though he looked kind of agitated with me. I hoped he could see that I was feeling better and would just let it go, at least for a while.

After another lengthy silence, Dan said, "I better get you home, or Rawdy will be out looking for me. He already thinks I'm strange. He thinks I'm a freak." Dan was chuckling.

"No! Rawdy doesn't think you're a *freak*." At least I was hoping that he did not.

"It's okay. I don't mind that they think I'm a freak."

"Really? Why not?"

"Well, I guess I don't care what any of them think of me. I know who I am, and I don't need their approval."

"Seriously?"

"Yeah!"

I could not understand. How can you not care what other people think of you? It was such a foreign thought to me. I did not know how to respond. We were silent until we got to my house. Sure enough, Dan had been right; Rawdy was sitting on my front porch swing waiting for us.

"Jerk!" I mumbled under my breath. I was shocked when Dan said, "He's not a jerk. He cares about you." Then Dan put his hand on my shoulder. I think I stopped breathing for a second, and I realized I was staring at his hand on my shoulder. He was touching me! Yes!

Dan followed my gaze and quickly removed his hand.

"I know there was something you were going to tell me this afternoon, but for whatever reason, you didn't feel like you could; I want you to know I'm not going to push you on the subject. Understand you're not alone, and anytime you want to talk, I'll be here. There's nothing, and I mean *nothing*, you could ever say that would change the way I feel about you...I mean think of you. So *if* you feel like...no, I mean *when* you feel like you can trust me, then I'll be waiting to listen. Now you better go before Rawdy comes over here and pulls you out of my car."

Rawdy was still sitting motionless on the swing, but I saw the intensity in his face that Dan had noticed. Rawdy was gripping the swing so hard that I was sure he would leave imprints.

Dan and I parted without saying another word. It was strange, but it almost seemed like he knew how alone, how scared, and how freakish I felt. But as appealing as that would be, it was impossible. While it is true that small towns know everyone's business, what was bothering me had never been made known to anyone in this town, not even my aunt or Rawdy knew why we left California.

Rawdy interrupted my thoughts with a loud yell. "Get over here!"

"What are you doing here?"

"I was waiting on you. What took you so long?"

"We were just talking. He's a very nice guy."

"Ruthy, he's one of those FFJ's and I don't ever want you hanging out with him or his friends again. Okay?"

"No! It's not okay. If I want to hang out with him or his friends, I will. You are not the boss of me. And what's an FFJ?"

"Freaks, Ruthy, they're all freaks, and you don't need to be hanging around them!"

There was that word again. "Why would you call him a freak, and why did he know you would call him that?"

"Because that's what they are. Freaks! I don't remember the rest of their name. We all just call them freaks." He paused for a moment and added, "I have to make one exception–Sarah is not like all the rest, and I don't mind if you hang with her."

When Rawdy mentioned Sarah's name, his mouth turned up with a shy little smile, and his voice became much softer. I had never realized that he had a soft spot for her.

Just then my dad drove into the driveway. Rawdy looked at me and said, "I mean it, Ruthy, stay away from them." Then he gentled down, gave me a hug, and kissed the top of my head saying, "I want you to be happy and safe."

By the time my dad got to the porch, Rawdy was on the second step.

"Hi, Dad!"

"Hey, kids. What's up?"

"Hey, Uncle Eli, I was just heading out."

"Rawdy, you don't have to go because I showed up."

"No, it isn't that at all. I'm already late, thanks to Ruthy here." He sneered at me and continued saying, "Some of the guys and I help out a local farmer with his pumpkin patch, or I should say, pumpkin field. Mr. Findlay always says, 'You can't call twenty acres a patch. It's a field, boy.' One of the other guys will be pulling double duty to take up my slack."

"That sounds like a great experience for you. I'd say that'll be quite the character builder."

"Yeah. It's a true test of humility. Mr. Findlay and his hired hand each take a row and cut the ripe pumpkins off of the dead vines. Then one guy drives the truck and wagon with two guys in the wagon. Four of us taller guys walk alongside the wagon and pick up the pumpkins, tossing them to the guys in the wagon. We get paid a fair wage, but we are docked pay if we drop and bust any pumpkins. It's all in preparation for the Findlay's big Pumpkin Fest. Everyone in town goes to buy their pumpkins, and they have hayrides and fresh apple cider. It's always held the last Saturday in October, you know, the week of Halloween."

I had never heard of Hallo...whatever he said, and I was tired of the conversation, so I headed into the house. I was sure Dad would force me to go to this, but I was still upset over Rawden's judgment against Dan and his friends.

Rawdy left, and Dad came into the house. I noticed Dad had brought home fried chicken for dinner. We ate without saying much. I did not feel like talking, and for some reason Dad was not forcing me into a conversation. After dinner, Dad settled down in front of his TV for a night of football. I started to head up to my room when he called my name.

"Ruthy, could you come here a minute?"

"What is it, Dad?"

"I've been meaning to ask you how you're doing—with school and all."

"It's okay."

"Did you make any friends?"

"Yeah, actually, there were a few kids that I really enjoyed hanging out with."

"Really? I hope Rawdy is one of those."

"You know he's like my brother."

I thought Dad was finished, so I headed toward the stairs, but he stopped me once again.

"Ruthy?"

"Yeah, Dad?"

"I want you to know that you don't have to try to make me happy. You've been taking care of me far too long, and I want you to be a kid again–one who's able to have some fun."

"I don't mind taking care of you."

"I know. Honey, please don't worry about me. This has been a hard year for both of us, and I know you've…well, you've really been trying to make me happy. Ruth, it isn't your responsibility to protect me. I'm the parent, and I need to start taking care of you. I love you, kiddo."

I walked over to his chair and gave him a kiss on his cheek and replied, "I love you too, Daddy."

I headed back up the stairs, but once again Dad stopped me.

"Ruthy?"

"Yes, Dad."

"Just be careful who you share your secrets with."

"What do you mean? Is there someone that I should be worried about?"

"No, of course not. Isn't it time for you to go to bed?" Dad was short with his answer, and anytime he says, "Go to bed," marks the end of the conversation.

I went to my room and tried to listen to music, but all I could think of were Rawdy's comments about the *"freaks."* It was strange, but I felt that for the first time I could identify. I am a freak, but surely that was not what Rawdy meant. Could these kids be like me? Can they read minds too? Impossible.

I desperately desired to tell Dan what had happened in California–why we had left so quickly, and what a weird person I was. I knew that I did the right thing trying to protect my dad, but I wished there was someone I could talk to. I had tried talking about it to Rawdy once, but he could not understand, and now my dad's words were fresh in my mind: "It's not your responsibility to protect me". I believe he was trying to convince me that it was okay to get close to someone, to share my life with someone–someone besides him. Someone such as Dan? At least that is what I hoped he was saying.

How could I ever consider telling Dan who I really was? My own father did not want to talk about it–it could not be easy for Dad. I knew at times he must have thought I was a freak too. Who other than a freak could knowingly let their friend commit suicide?

3

Episodes

The following two weeks passed rather slowly. Dan and I sat together every day at lunch, and he was graciously tutoring me two days a week–not that I really needed his help. I was hoping by that point we would be dating, but we were no closer. We mostly talked about homework. Life was fairly dull with little excitement, that is, until the last Friday of October.

Friday was a pep assembly, and all the students were allowed to miss their last hour of class for the assembly; most teachers were not even in their classrooms. I went straight from class to the bleachers, looking for the perfect seat, next to Dan of course, but I could not find him.

I settled for a seat next to Sarah and a few of her friends. I decided to ask Sarah if she knew where Dan was.

I leaned close to Sarah's ear and said, "Where's Dan?" But we were sitting so close to the band that she could not hear a single word. Sarah, looking confused, pointed to her ear. I tried shouting, but right at the moment I said Dan's name, the band went completely silent. Everyone within an ear's shot glared at me with evident disdain. I was so embarrassed. After the team ran a short scrimmage, we all stood up, and I tried once more to ask Sarah if she knew where Dan was, but before I could get the words out, the crowd parted, and there he was standing, looking straight at me.

It seemed impossible to think I could ever get used to how magnificent Dan's eyes were, or how truly GQ-like his face was. He looked like a movie star, and yet he was staring right into my eyes and smiling directly at me. He was staring at me! We started walking toward each other, but before I could hear his voice I saw his lips mouth, *"Ruthy"*–my heart skipped a beat in exhilaration. I was captivated by this man–he was my dream at night and my smile by day. I had never felt that way before. I had always loved to sleep, mostly to dream of a better life, but now even the dreams were not as good as reality. I could not wait to wake up in the morning and see his face again.

"Ruthy, would you go with me...to get an ice cream?"

"I would *love* to go with you!" I was trying to keep from embarrassing myself by appearing too desperate for his company, but I was sure my face was giving me away. My eyes were wide open, and for some insane reason, I could not stop giggling.

"Here, we can go this way." Dan put his hand on my lower back and escorted me through the crowd. I tensed the second he touched me, but I hoped he would not take it as a sign of reluctance. My senses were in overload by his touch.

"Where were you during the rally, Dan?"

"Oh, it was nothing really. I just had to make up a quiz that I'll miss Monday."

"You're not going to be here Monday?" My heart began to fail due to disappointment.

"I'm going to be late to school Monday, but I plan to be back by lunch. Can you save me a seat?"

Sheer relief started my heart beating again. "Sure!"

"Ruthy, I was hoping that you and I could find some time to talk today...alone."

"I don't have any plans tonight so...so I am yours."

He glanced down at me with a big smile and said, "Good."

We were the only students at the ice cream shop. I was nervous, and Dan seemed to be quieter than usual. If we continued like that, our afternoon would be very long, but unproductive. Dan remembered what I ordered the last time and got me a vanilla Dr. Pepper and two chocolate, chocolate dipped cones, one for me and one for him. Eating that cone was a bit of a trick. The chocolate ice cream is softer than vanilla, and the ice cream starts melting the second the hot dipping chocolate hits it. So when you take your first bite and break open the hard chocolate shell, the melted ice cream starts dripping immediately. I was thankful that I hadn't worn a white shirt today–I had a tendency to drip on my shirt, and chocolate is not easy to get out of white! I have ruined several of my favorite shirts. I was somewhat pleased when Dan dripped ice cream on his shirt and his pants. I did not want him to ruin his shirt, but it meant that I was not the only klutz. I giggled out loud and could tell it embarrassed him, but it did not seem to distract him long.

After we finished our cones, Dan suggested we walk to the lake. The walk was very pleasant, and it was another gorgeous day. It was a slightly cooler day–close to seventy degrees, but not quite–and the trees were in full, fall color. We walked down a gravel lane where the trees arched over the road, creating a canopy. The green leaves were all gone now, but here in Gilpinton there was an unusual abundance of crimson red leaves that seemed to create an air of romance. Dan was always a step ahead of me as we walked down the lane. I enjoyed being behind him; that way I could stare at his handsome body without him seeing.

I was a little chilled from the wind blowing through the trees, and I wrapped my arms around myself, trying to stay warm. We made small talk as we walked, commenting on the weather, school, and ice cream–the ice cream seemed like a mistake now. I could tell he wanted to say something, but I was not sure what he needed from me to make him feel comfortable enough to say it.

"Ruthy, do you need my hoodie?"

"No. I'll be fine."

"Sure?"

"Sure."

I would not have minded to wear his hoodie, but his hoodie was back in his car, and I did not want him leaving my side—even for a second. We finally reached the lake and found an old log to sit on. I was gazing to the right, taking in the majestic scenery, propped by my left hand resting on the log. Dan was sitting to my left, hunched forward, resting his arms on his knees and playing with his fingers. He was obviously nervous, making it painful to watch him, and just when I thought I could not take it any longer, I felt his right hand on top of my left hand. I fought with every fiber of my being to keep my eyes off of our hands. I slowly turned my head, making sure I would meet his gaze. I was concerned that he would feel uncomfortable and yank his hand away. Our eyes met, and I gingerly smiled, waiting for him to smile back. He did.

We had both apparently been holding our breath, and we let it out at the same time. The release of tension caused us to start laughing uncontrollably. When we were finally able to compose ourselves, we were staring into each other's eyes. Suddenly, silence filled the air.

Dan broke the silence with unexpected words. Dan said, "Ruthy, I have something to tell you, and I am sorry I've waited this long to bring it up, but I can't stand it any longer."

Dan and I had been eating lunch at the same table all week, and everyday we would spend most of the hour talking instead of eating. The conversations were never about anything important, but we had a bond that was almost unnatural. I could talk about anything to Dan, and he actually wanted to listen, and not just listen, he wanted to tell me everything too. Some of his topics were boring, but I did not mind because I was talking with Dan. Each day our conversations seemed to get easier and easier, we were definitely more relaxed with each other, but not now. Dan was obviously anxious about something, and it must be important.

I turned so I was facing him and moved my left hand so our palms were touching, then took my right hand and covered his. I laid all three of our hands on my left leg and said, "Dan, you can tell me anything."

"Yeah, I think I can!" His face lit up, and his anxiety appeared to melt away.

"Ruthy, I'm a member of a youth group called Freaks For Jesus, or FFJ for short."

"Oh...so that's what that stands for?"

Dan was in complete shock and said, "You've heard of it before?!"

"Well, just from Rawdy. I didn't think you looked like the farmer type."

"Farmer? Well, no, I'm not a farmer. Where did that come from?"

I laughed a little and explained, "The only FF anything I've ever heard of before is FFA–you know . . . the Future Farmers of America. I couldn't figure out what the "J" stood for, but that's the only group I could come up with in my head."

"Oh...no, it means Freaks For Jesus. Our youth leader came up with the name."

"But what exactly does it mean?"

He smiled and clarified the title. "The word freaks refers to a fanatic–somebody who is fanatical about something. So we, as FFJ's, are people who are fanatical about Jesus. Our lives revolve around our faith. I've been an FFJ since I turned thirteen. My parents are also believers of Jesus, as were their parents. I've really never known anything other than this life and our beliefs. We meet every week at our church with a group of about thirty other families; it's called the Gilpinton Community Gathering. We have a band that plays songs, and we worship by singing, dancing, clapping, bowing, kneeling, and raising our hands. These are all things which are spoken of in the words from God. We study the old and the new text. Sometimes we call it the Truth, or you might know it as the Old and New Testament."

Dan was sharing a lot of interesting and important information, but it was hard for me to concentrate. I had been told by Sarah that Dan could not sing, but it was hard to believe it as I sat there and listened to his melodious voice. Everything about Dan drew me closer to his side. I could hardly bear to listen to him any longer–I saw the tension rising as he tried to explain, and I needed to end his agony. Finally, I blurted out, "Dan, I'm an FFJ too! That's not what we were called, but I belonged to a gathering in California. They called it the Azusa Meetings. I only attended for a couple months, and I officially joined just weeks before I moved out here."

"Oh, Ruthy, I'm so happy!" Dan pulled his hand out of my grip and threw both arms around me in a vigorous embrace.

"I can't breathe! Dan, please loosen up a bit."

"Oh, I'm sorry! Did I hurt you?" He grabbed my shoulders and pushed me an arms length away, as if to examine the damage he had done.

I was disappointed that he had let go of me. I needed to remember to be more subtle next time.

"No, I'm fine. Please continue." I grabbed his right hand again and resumed my position.

He did not try to resist, but rather fell right back into the conversation. "You see...I've been such an idiot." Dan paused for a second before he continued chattering away. "I like you. But I was so worried you wouldn't agree with my beliefs that I didn't want to say anything to you, and that is so not like me. I'm usually the most radical of us radicals, but you said something that first day that led me to hope that maybe...just maybe, you were one of us. I felt it was a long shot, but I kept faith. You know there are only a few hundred thousand of us these days, and the probability of you being an FFJ was just so slim that I almost didn't want to let myself hope. How long have you known the Truth?"

"It's been less than three months."

"And your dad?"

"No."

Out of nowhere, that question brought up so many emotions; I started to cry. Whether it was really just about my dad, or the combination of all the nerves and anxiety of the day, I really did not know, but nevertheless, my emotions had gotten the best of me–it certainly was not the first time. Dad called them "episodes." This one was the worst that Dan had seen so far. It seemed impossible to stop.

Dan was so thoughtful; he pulled me over against his chest and patted my back. "It'll be okay, Ruthy. If you don't like me, we can just be friends."

Could he really think that I did not like him? I croaked out the words, "Of course I like you."

"That's nice to hear. I thought you did, but I'm not good at this kind of thing."

I was still crying when Dan said, "I know it's been hard, but you're not alone anymore, and you don't have to be strong for anyone else. Just let it out. Don't be afraid to cry. I'd dare to say you've not really mourned losing your family, the loss of your mom, and I know...well, I know California holds some nightmares."

Seriously, could this guy be any more perfect? He actually wanted me to cry, to "let it all out", and not even just that, he was also explaining to me why I was bawling my eyes out on the most perfect day of my life. I hadn't even been sure why I was crying until he explained it. But he was right. I had been so concerned with my dad, that I had not allowed myself to consider how much it hurt me–it did hurt...it hurt a lot. I think that was why I had episodes. I had bottled up my emotions until I could not take it anymore and they came exploding out.

I had so much phlegm that I could hardly breathe, and the words were hard to speak, but I had to say it. No one else would have understood or even allowed me to say it, but right then in that moment I knew that Dan would be a safe place for my thoughts to land.

"If I am so hopelessly flawed...that my own mother can't love me, then who can? I mean a lot of parents get divorced, but most kids end up with their mom, especially the daughters. My mother said she was done being a wife, and she was done being a mom— my mom. I don't even know where she is or how to get a hold of her. She cared more about getting her half of their property than she cared about me." When I finished the words, the rest of my emotions came flooding out. My body was shaking, and snot was starting to run down my face–it was so nasty.

Dan reached into his pocket, like a good country boy, he always had a red handkerchief in his back pocket. He picked up my face and gently wiped my nose. "Blow," he commanded. I willingly obliged him and blew my nose. Disgusting.

He picked a clean corner of the handkerchief and wiped my eyes. Then he said, "Well, I don't know why your mother left your father, and I don't know why she didn't want the joys of being a mother any longer, but you are completely wrong when you say, 'If my own mother can't love me then who can?' The operative word there being 'can't'. That would imply there is something wrong with you, and there is absolutely nothing wrong with you that could keep anyone from being able to love you. Now, maybe you could say that your mother doesn't love you anymore, or isn't willing to love you, but you are utterly wrong with the use of the word *can't*. It's important that you understand why this has nothing to do with your lack of lovability, because you're not the one with the problem, my dear. It's your mother and her ability, or willingness, to love. There is nothing about you that could hinder someone else's ability to love you, believe me, and I will prove it."

I pulled away and said, "Be serious. How can you prove that?"

I expected Dan to hold me tighter or speak soothing words, but instead he tried to debate with me, which was somewhat ticking me off. I just wanted him to listen to me–not fix me.

"I don't know him real well, but from what I can see, your father loves you very much."

"Yeah, I know!"

"And then there's Rawdy...he also loves you very much."

"In a love/hate kind of relationship, like with brothers and sisters." I giggled a little after that statement. My irritation had started to fade, and I knew he was trying to help me. How could I be upset with him? He was so cute.

"But most of all..."

Oh...my...goodness! Is he really going to say it? Is he going to tell me he loves me? *Breathe, Ruthy, breathe.*

"Most of all, Jesus loves you."

"Oh...well, yes, of course I do believe that." I *was* glad he had mentioned Jesus, but I was disappointed that he had not included himself in that explanation. He was right, and it made me feel a little better. I was sitting straight up with my hands in my lap, looking at my finger nails, trying to figure what to say or do next.

Dan broke the silence by saying, "I hope you don't think I've made light of what you said. But, Ruthy, you must not take for granted the love of Jesus. Jesus paid the highest price–He gave His life–but first He left His father's side. He was in Heaven, where we all want to be, and He gave it all up to come down here so we could know the love of God, our Father. Jesus said, 'Greater love has no one than this, that he lay down his life for his friends.' That is exactly what He did for you."

I did not look up when I answered, "Oh, no! I don't feel that you took what I said lightly. I've come to know how real Jesus is and how much He loves me, but I haven't ever told anyone about my mom, and frankly, no one…well, no one really ever cared to listen. You are just so incredibly kind to listen to me."

"Ruthy, I do care about you, but I don't know you well enough to tell you that I love you." He could see the look on my face, which told him he better explain a little more and fast. "Of course I do love you, in a way, and I care about you, more than just as a friend, but I will only tell the woman I'm going to marry that I love her." He took hold of my hands and said, "Neither of us is ready for that kind of declaration."

There was an extended period of total silence, and I felt I better end it before neither one of us could. "Wow! Things just got really awkward, didn't they?" I started a deep belly laugh at that thought, and Dan soon joined in.

"I didn't mean to go there. I knew you were wondering why I didn't put my name in there as someone who loved you…"

"You did? How?"

"Well, I assumed that you did, and then it just got awkward. Plus, Jesus' love is way more important than my love for you because His love will never let you down. I can't say the same for mine. "

"I know…His love is all that has kept me going this past month."

"I think we should start heading back. It'll be dark in another hour."

We headed back to his car. Halfway there Dan said, "Ruthy, do you think you could share with me about California?"

"Dan, that's a long story, and my dad will be getting worried if I'm out too late. Would you mind taking me back to my house?"

"No. I don't mind, and I understand if you aren't ready to tell me the story."

"It's okay. I'll tell you everything when we get to my house."

4

Then Death

By the time we walked back to Dan's car and drove to my house, it was practically dark. Dan and I stepped in my front door. Dad was in his usual spot (sitting in his recliner watching television), so I informed him we would be out on the porch swing. Before we walked out of the house, I fiddled around in my purse and pulled out a folded piece of paper, then grabbed a fleece blanket off the couch.

Dan had a quizzical look on his face when he asked, "What's that for, Ruthy?"

"Once the sun goes down, the temperature will drop down to the low fifties, and I know this conversation is going to take a while."

We walked from the lake to his car holding hands. Then in the car he had taken my hand again, but we were not holding hands in front of my dad, or now as we walked to the swing. I was hoping he would take my hand once we sat down. If not, I was going to grab his. I needed some kind of physical touch to reassure me as I recounted the story of these past three months–the day Jacob died. We both sat on the swing; it was small enough that we were sitting shoulder to shoulder. We took the blanket and draped it over our legs, and I put both of my hands in my lap on top of the blanket.

Dan was fidgeting with the blanket, tucking us both in, and then he looked at me and said, "Okay, you may begin...now."

I was feeling extremely self-conscious and had every intention of grabbing his hand, but for some reason I could not do it. My mind kept messing with me. *What will he think? Maybe he does not want to hold my hand.* We had been holding hands most of the afternoon, but at that moment in time I felt like we had started all over again, like a new day. It took me a second to compose myself and decide what to do, or how to begin.

"I–I–I don't know..." I stuttered while trying to focus my thoughts.

Dan had a strange look on his face, as if he doubted I would ever tell him the story. But just when I thought I could not go on, he said, "Oh, I'm sorry," and he grabbed my right hand, cradling it between both of his hands. "Now you can begin. Sorry, I was wondering what you were waiting for."

"How do you do that?" I smiled at him and began to tell the story.

"Dad decided that California would be a great place to make a new start. It was mostly just the farthest thing from Nebraska. We had finally sold all the property and divided up the profits with Mom, when Dad got a call from an old buddy saying he had a construction job near the beach. Dad jumped at the offer, and we were headed out in just two days."

I paused for a second and adjusted the blanket before I began again.

"Being in California was hard at first. I'd lived in the same house as long as I could remember, not to mention in the same state. I'd known all of my friends since we started walking. Then there was the fact that my mom was gone, and I was alone with my dad."

Dan compassionately said, "That must have been hard for you."

"Yeah, it was, but we had only been there two weeks when one of my teachers asked me to come to her house for a gathering. She said, 'Ruthy, come and hear the Truth.' I had no clue what she was talking about, but for some reason I went."

"That is *so* cool! I wish more people would be so bold," Dan exclaimed.

"I recognized a few kids from my school, and I enjoyed myself so much that I started going every week. After a month, I officially joined their group. I thought I'd understood what they were talking about, but it wasn't until that night when I joined that I really understood. I guess no one can really understand when they're on the outside looking in–there just isn't anything else in the world like Jesus or the Holy Spirit."

"That is *so* true. I remember when I first asked Jesus to be my Lord and Redeemer. It was as if I had been walking around wearing sunglasses and earphones. Everything I looked at and everything I heard was muted. I had been reading the Word of God, and I had been hearing the teachings and songs, but it wasn't until I decided to live my life for Jesus that I could understand the true meaning of the words. Suddenly the teachings and songs made complete sense. I totally understood."

"Dan, I completely agree, but if you keep interrupting me, I'll never get through this story." I smiled at him in an attempt to soften the strength of my words.

"Okay. I'm sorry. I'll try not to interrupt again. It's just very exciting."

Watching his enthusiasm made me giggle. He looked like a little kid who had just opened a present.

I continued my story saying, "I'd heard old myths about these people of faith, but I never thought they were real. I mean it just goes against everything science teaches us, and that's all most of us have ever heard. I know most people don't believe science has anything to do with faith or beliefs, but that is what science is. Science starts as a hypothesis, and a hypothesis is just someone's theory, which is a guess that is based on their beliefs. What is a hypothesis but someone's guess, assumption, *belief*? And that is where all science begins. After a month of attending the gathering, I was discovering that many of my former assumptions were wrong.

"Most of the kids from the gathering were in my school, and that made life easier being in such a strange and foreign place. I ended up with a friend in every class, and four of my best friends were in the same lunch hour with me. Things were going great until the end of September. I had befriended a young man who didn't have any other friends. Black was his color of choice, which is a very strange color to wear in such a sunny state. He stayed to himself, and most of the teachers didn't even talk to him or even call on him. I noticed that he usually got B+ or higher on tests.

"I guess the teachers thought that he wasn't giving them trouble and was doing okay in class, so they should just leave him alone–he looked very intimidating. I think *everyone* thought they should leave him alone, which for me, is usually my signal to butt in.

"From day one at Bayside High, I'd made it my challenge to get Jacob to talk to me. It took over a month, but he did finally start talking to me. It unexpectedly started one day. He walked into geometry class and said, 'Hi, Ruth.' That was all, but it was a start, and I was hooked. I had to get him to say more. That day, at lunch, I walked right over to his table–I say 'his table' because no one ever sat at the table with him–and sat down right across from him. I could hear all the chatter around us from people who were astonished that I'd be sitting with Jacob–most people were scared of him, but not me. Little did I know then, but they were right. Jacob looked up from his plate and started shaking his head and laughing. That was the first and only time I saw him laugh. I asked him what was so funny, but he just said, 'Ruth, you never stop amazing me.' That was the only time I sat at his table, but it had done its job. We began hanging out and having full conversations.

"Jacob and I even went to a movie once. I tried to get him involved in other activities and with some of my other friends, but neither side really seemed to want that. Jacob said, 'Ruth, I like being a loner. You're already putting a cramp in my style. I don't need any other losers hanging around.' And my other friends were terrified of him. For a few weeks I enjoyed my accomplishment of befriending the most unfriendly person in the school, but then the worst thing ever happened.

"It was a Monday morning, and I woke up with laryngitis. I wasn't supposed to be at school that day because all the choir students were going to district contest. I was supposed to be singing "Ave Maria" at 11:00 a.m., but that didn't happen since I had laryngitis and couldn't even talk above a whisper. I had a good shot at getting a "I+" at contest. It was driving me crazy sitting around the apartment thinking about the lost opportunity, so I went to school. When I walked in the front door, Jacob was standing right there. The look on his face was that of sheer terror. I asked him if he was okay--or at least I attempted to ask--and he just kept saying, 'You aren't supposed to be here today, not today of all days, Ruth!'

"'What's wrong, Jacob?' I was able to hiss the few words. 'I have laryngitis if you can't tell.'

"'Shut up, Ruth!' Jacob yelled.

"'No, really, I'm sick and can't talk above a whisper. I'm not trying to pretend.' I noticed that even though I couldn't talk, for some reason I just kept trying to say more and more. Then I realized he didn't mean that as in, 'Oh shut up...you don't say,' but rather he meant it as in, 'Shut up, Ruthy...will you stop talking already?!'

"And that's when it happened. I knew what he was thinking. He had a gun!"

"A gun!" Dan spurted out. "I'm sorry; it just came out. I couldn't stop myself." I looked at him with disappointment. I was not happy he'd interrupted my story...again. I resumed where I had left off without further acknowledging his comment.

"I said, 'Jacob, what are you going to do with a gun?' He looked at me like I had just slapped him senseless.

"He said, 'Who said anything about a gun, Ruth? I didn't say I had a gun. Who said I had a gun? Because they're--they're lying to you.'

"I replied, 'No one told me you have a gun. But I'm right, you do have a gun. Jacob, who are you going to shoot?'

"Then I heard the thought and knew. I had to stop him, but how? I tried to reason with him, but whatever had made him snap was still very much in control. He just kept saying, 'She wasn't supposed to be here today. Not today!' as if he was talking to someone or something.

"I decided to run to the principal's office and tell him. Why would he believe me? I had no proof, but I had to try. Mr. Grandfield protested saying, 'Ruthy, you can't just make accusations like that.'

"'But if it's true, a lot of people are in danger. You have to do something!'

"'What am I supposed to do?' he asked.

"'Call him in here and check his stuff.'

"'Ruthy, people today are ready to sue over the littlest things, and I'm about to retire next year. Yes, Jacob is a loner, but that doesn't mean he would kill anyone.' Mr. Grandfield was trying to talk one of us into believing him–it wasn't going to be me.

"I could see I wasn't getting anywhere with him, so I tried the vice principal, and she just looked at me and called in the school nurse. 'Ruthy, you have a temperature of one hundred and two degrees, dear. You need to go home right now. Why on earth did you come to school?' Nurse Miller gently sat me in a chair as she read the thermometer. 'Dear, I am going to call your father.'

"My dad was off on a job and couldn't be reached, so my emergency contact, our next door neighbor, came and picked me up. I couldn't say anything to her; she was a sweet older woman, but I had barely talked to her before that day. She brought us homemade bread when we first moved in, and one day Dad asked her if she would be my emergency contact. He explained that all she would have to do is bring me home, and I'd be fine alone. I was rarely ever physically ill, and Dad never thought she'd be needed. On the other hand, I frequently have episodes and need some alone time.

"The vice-principal and the nurse were all sure I was just delusional because of the fever. I knew what I knew, but what was I going to do? What could I do? So I called the local police department and told them I thought a boy at school had a gun. They asked me if I'd seen the gun, and I had to tell them, 'No.' They asked if the boy had told me he had a gun, and I had to say, 'No.' Finally, the police officer told me that he would call the school and talk with the principal. I knew right then that this was a waste of time. I sat down on the couch and the next thing I knew, I was waking up in my bed–Dad must have put me there. I could hear the television from the living room. I got out of bed and started walking. The closer I got to the TV, the more I could hear of the horrifying story the news was reporting. The anchor woman plainly stated, 'A sixteen year old male, Jacob Smith, has fatally shot himself at Bayside High. Smith was in the cafeteria during lunch break when he stood up on a table and screamed, 'Not today! Why today?' He then took a hand gun out of his pocket and shot himself.'

"Dad was visibly shaken by the news, but he didn't know that I had any connection to Jacob, and I certainly wasn't going to tell him now. I stayed home from school the next day, and the next day they cancelled classes for Jacob's memorial. I couldn't see why they would cancel classes because he was friends with no one. Well, no one but me. My dad couldn't understand why I would want to go to his memorial, but I had to go, and I didn't see any easy way of explaining to Dad. I didn't want him to think I was any more of a freak than he already thought.

"We walked through the main entrance and straight into the auditorium. I never looked anyone in the eye, even though I felt everyone looking at me and heard several people whisper my name. The service was about an hour. Our choir sang a couple of songs, and the superintendent gave a short speech. When it was over, I headed to my locker. I needed my history book for an exam. When I opened my locker door, a note was stuck between the vent slats. It was a single sheet of ruled notebook paper with my name written on the outside–inside was a handwritten note. I quickly looked to the end for a signature, and there, to my horror, was Jacob's name."

This was the time to show Dan the note. I reached into my pocket and pulled out the paper I had gotten out of my purse. I unfolded it and handed it to Dan. "Here...read it for yourself," I said.

Talking about Jacob and what had happened caused pressure on my heart. I actually felt it. I wondered if a teenager could have a heart attack from telling a story. Our street was quiet in those few moments...not a single car or person went by. The silence was deafening. I was not sure if, or for how long, I could keep myself from a breakdown.

Ruth,

I can't believe you were at school today. I was sure you were going to be gone to that contest. I had made up my mind that today was the day, and I had to follow through. You have to know you can't stop me, if not today, then another day.

After I saw you, I knew that I couldn't do what I had planned. I couldn't risk hurting you. You're the only person who has ever been kind to me. Then I saw you go into Mr. G's office, and I panicked. I decided right then that I was only going to kill myself and not risk you being in the way.

So, I guess you can feel a little satisfaction that because you came to school today, 20 or so people will be alive tomorrow.
Sorry for letting you down, but thanks for being my friend.

Jacob

I gave him time to read the note, but before he could say anything, I started telling the rest of the story. "I was starting to get annoyed. There was an unbelievably loud noise. I tried to find the source, without success. I looked up and saw several people staring at me. I realized then that the noise was someone screaming. I couldn't figure out why no one was trying to stop the screaming. They were just staring at me. I kept looking at their faces for help, and then I knew: I was the person screaming. I fell down to the floor and assumed the fetal position. My dad knelt down beside me and so did Principal Grandfield. They picked me up and took me into the office.

"I was finally able to stop screaming and calmed myself down. I saw my dad reading the note and heard Mr. Grandfield explaining that he hadn't believed me. After what seemed like hours, Dad walked over to the leather couch where I was sitting and knelt in front of me. He took hold of my face and said, 'Ruthy, you knew this boy?'"

I looked at Dan and asked, "Seriously, was that the most important question at that moment? I've often thought it was odd that he asked me that. I expected him to comfort me. Why? I don't know. He never tried to after Mom left."

I did not let Dan respond, but instead I continued with the story. "I curtly answered my dad saying, 'Yes, Dad, I knew Jacob. He was...my friend.' My anger was evident in my voice, which was still a little hoarse from the lingering laryngitis. I wasn't really mad at Dad, or even Jacob. I was mad at me.

"Dad redeemed himself by saying, 'Honey, I'm sorry. I can't believe you didn't tell me you knew him. We even watched the story on the news. You must have been crushed, and if you'd known that he had a gun...' Before he could finish, I interrupted saying, 'I should have been able to stop him, right?'

"'No! Oh, Ruthy!' He grabbed me around my neck and hugged me as he said my name. 'Ruthy, I'm just happy you weren't hurt.' I could barely breathe because of his Stetson cologne. I couldn't tell him what I was really thinking. Dad's not a believer, and he wouldn't understand. I knew Jacob had a gun. So, why didn't I ever tell him about Jesus? Wasn't I supposed to be a Christian? Isn't that what we as Christians are supposed to do? Isn't that what the words from God say? We are supposed to 'go ye into all the world' proclaiming the Truth. How could I let someone kill himself, knowing he was going to end up in hell? I'd been trying to convince myself that I was working up to telling Jacob. I needed to befriend him first and let him see the love of Jesus shining through me. Then I'd help him know the Truth–know Jesus. Now it's too late–Jacob is dead."

"You can't blame yourself," Dan whispered.

I heard Dan, but I didn't acknowledge his comment. Instead, I continued saying, "As I was mentally beating myself up, Dad and Mr. Grandfield started arguing. Dad was defending me. 'Mr. Grandfield, you will not put the blame on my daughter. She came to you with this information. You're the one to blame.'

"Mr. Grandfield countered saying, 'Well, she knew of the gun, and that makes her responsible.'

"Mr. Grandfield was trying to construct a defense for himself, but Dad was not going to stand for that. 'You said yourself that she told you she hadn't seen a gun, and that he didn't tell her he had a gun, so how is she to blame? She couldn't know for sure that he had a gun.' Dad's face was a deep crimson red, and sweat rings were starting to form under his arms.

"Mr. Grandfield continued saying, 'Exactly, Eli, how did your daughter know he had a gun? Why did she think there was danger? That is unless she's one of those freaks.'

"With that statement, Dad swung around with his fist up ready to hit Mr. Grandfield, but he didn't. He stopped himself and looked down at the floor. 'Ruthy, lets go! Mr. Grandfield, my daughter will no longer be attending your school. We're moving to Missouri.'

"'Missouri!' Mr. Grandfield and I both said in unison.

"'I have family there, and it's a much safer place to live.' With those words, my dad grabbed my arm and pulled me out of the room.

"Dad and I never said another word about the events of that day. I tried once while we were packing, but he was emphatic saying, 'Ruthy, I don't ever want to talk about that again. There is nothing wrong with you. You are not a freak.' But here I am, a month later, and that word is in my face again. I was a freak. I am a freak. How did I know that Jacob had a gun? To my knowledge, I've never experienced anything like that before, and I don't know how it worked that time. I heard the thought in my head, like a voice was speaking to me, but the voice sounded like my own voice. I have my suspicions. I think it might have something to do with the gatherings I'd been frequenting and the Truth. But, after Jacob's suicide, I hadn't been able to get back to the gathering, nor had I seen any of my friends at Jacob's memorial. Dad had us packing the second we got home, and we left California four days after our meeting with Mr. Grandfield. There'd been no time to talk with anyone who might be able to explain why I knew Jacob had a gun."

"Dan, are you still listening to me?" I was pretty sure he had fallen asleep.

"Yes...yes," he said clearing his throat. "You are a very perceptive person, Ruthy. That must have been awful for you. I'm so sorry that you have to bear the weight of this tragedy, but I hope you understand that the whole Jacob thing wasn't your fault, nor could you have stopped him." He was yawning when he finished his sentence.

I could not help myself and yawned too. I looked at my watch and noticed that it was almost midnight. Tomorrow was the Pumpkin Fest, and my dad wanted to get an early start. This was going to be a very short night.

"Ruthy, I hate to leave you, but I have a big day tomorrow. I've got to get some rest."

We both stood up, and Dan grabbed my shoulders. "I want you to understand I think you did all the right things trying to stop Jacob, and I'm sorry you had to live through such an experience."

It was obvious that Dan was concerned about me, and I was afraid he was going to stand around talking for another hour. "Yeah, I know. I also understand that you need to get home, but your concern for my feelings is keeping you from going. So . . . I'm giving you permission to go home and get some rest. I'll be fine. Are you sure you're able to drive home?"

"No problem. I live just outside of town. I'll be home in five minutes, tops."

He gave me a short hug and then opened the front door. I was standing inside, watching him walk down the stairs, when he suddenly turned around and said, "Sweet dreams, Ruthy. I'll see you Monday." He took a couple more steps then said, "Oh, and don't forget to save me a seat at lunch."

5

Pumpkin Fest

The last day of October came with much fanfare for this little town. This was the big day: farmer Findlay's Pumpkin Fest. Dad decided I needed a distraction, so we were going to go drink apple cider and pick out a pumpkin.

This place had some strange traditions. What did Rawdy call it? Hallowon...maybe. I had never seen anything like it. Back in Nebraska, we were very isolated on the farm. Most everyone in Gilpinton goes to the party, then they all go home with a pumpkin that they purchased from farmer Findlay and set it on their front porch. After an hour or so, all the small children go door-to-door, knocking and asking for candy. Interesting.

It looks to me that Mr. Findlay has a good thing going because not only does he sell the pumpkins, he also owns the only candy store in town. I cannot believe my dad is actually going along with this silly tradition, but he is. Mom never would have allowed us to attend these kinds of things.

At first the Pumpkin Fest did not appear to be very interesting, and unfortunately, it never got much better. There were a lot of old people and even more little kids. I scanned the crowd. I did not want it to be obvious that I was looking for someone, but my dad noticed and seemed a little too happy about it.

Dan was not at the festival, and neither were any of his usual friends, not even Sarah was there. We saw my aunt and uncle, and a few neighbors, but I did not make much conversation. The highlight of the afternoon was a three-legged race with Mike. Mike found me at the festival and talked me into being his partner. He had explained to me that there was a prize of a gift card worth twenty dollars–I could use it to download more songs onto my iPod. I reluctantly agreed to the race and was sorely disappointed in our performance.

Mike and I had been in the lead for the first three fourths of the race, but at the last minute he looked down and stared at me, moving us off course, and pushing me into the lane of our nearest competitors. My free leg and another competitor's leg tangled and down the four of us went!

"Mike, I'm so sorry. I can be a klutz sometimes."

"Don't worry about it, Ruthy. It was really my fault. I lost focus. You have nothing to be sorry about. You have pretty eyes."

"Thanks. I guess."

The race only lasted a total of sixty seconds from start to finish, and I did not stick around long. Mike was acting strange. I decided to go find my dad.

"Hey, Dad. What are you drinking?"

"Hey, Ruthy. It's hot apple cider, and it is delicious. You should try some."

I grabbed a cup. The apple cider was really good. I decided to get the warm apple cider with a cinnamon stick floating in the cup. It was an aromatic treat.

As if someone had rang a bell, the entire crowd dispersed at exactly 8:00 p.m. Dad needed to pick up something from Aunt Marge's house, so we arrived home around eight-thirty, and then all the little kids came knocking on the door. I had not realized the kids would be dressed up in costumes. Most of them were dressed like cartoon characters.

There was a much harder knock on the door at nine o'clock. I thought I recognized that knock. "Rawdy, what are you doing? Aren't you a little old for dress up?"

"Ah, Ruthy, it's our senior year, and…well…we like candy."

It was not until he said *"we"* that I noticed there were three, very large, cartoon characters standing at my door. I had to laugh. "You guys look ridiculous!" I was not sure I knew who the other two were, but the big one was most likely Mike.

"Well, Ruthy, we have to run. People stop handing out candy at 9:30 sharp, and I'm determined to fill my pillow sack before then."

The big guy was holding a bat, but he was dressed as a gray, fuzzy rabbit. I took a chance and said, "Mike, why do you have a bat?"

Mike leaned in the door to whisper his answer to me. "There's another tradition to this night, and this is…well, one of my tools."

I copied Mike's actions and leaned forward to whisper, "What tradition?"

It was Rawdy that spoke this time in his normal volume and said, "Don't worry about it." Rawdy shot a disapproving look at Mike. I do not think Rawdy ever intended for me to know about this other tradition. Then as fast as they had come, they were gone.

At ten o'clock, I went upstairs to my room to get ready for bed. I got into my pajamas and realized that I did not have my iPod…

again. I sat on the edge of the bed trying to remember when I had used it last. Oh, yeah! I had it in the car on the way home from the festival. I should have guessed in the car because every time I get into the car Dad wants to make small talk, and I just end up taking it out of my ears and turning it off. I rummaged around under my bed looking for my flip flops. I found one brown one, and then I pulled out a blue one. I thought for a minute; one was a left, and one was a right. Who would see me? I was only going to run down and get my iPod out of the car. That would take all of a minute. So I steadied myself on the desk while I slipped on my mismatched flip flops.

When I got to the door I noticed that it seemed darker than usual outside, yet the moon was bright, and there were no clouds. I turned on my porch light and ran out to the car. I had failed to realize when I was considering the mismatched shoes that the brown one had a wedge heel while the blue one was completely flat. I was glad no one was around to see me hobble out to the car. I was shutting the car door when I heard a strange noise. I wanted to run to the house screaming, but in complete opposition to a sane reaction, I turned around and noticed that all the street lights on our block were off. That should have been when my brain and feet got in sync with each other, but no. My brain was saying, "Run!", but my feet would not move. I was frozen in place. I could hear voices and sounds like something being smashed. Like an idiot from a horror movie, I actually said something. "Who's there?" As if an ax murderer is going to say, "Oh, it's me...your friendly local ax murderer!"

To my surprise, someone did answer. "Ruthy, is that you?"

"Yes, who are you?"

Then another voice said, "Ruthy, get in your house. Now!"

I knew that voice. "Rawdy?"

"Dude, now we've had it. You should've just kept your mouth shut, and she wouldn't have known who we were."

"Mike, is that you?"

"Oh, would you both just shut up?!" Another voice spoke, but I was not able to tell who it was.

Rawdy spoke again, and I could tell he was walking closer. "Ruthy, I mean it. Go and get inside your house now. I'm not gonna tell you again. It's not safe for you out here."

I could tell by the intensity of his voice that he was not joking, and I did not want to push him too far, but before I could move he was standing right next to me. If I had not heard his voice, I would not have recognized him. He was dressed in black, and he even had black stripes strategically painted on his face. Rawdy took a hold of my left elbow and pulled me to my front door.

"What is up with you? Why are you walking like that? Is one of your legs hurting?" Before I could answer, we were at my front door, and the porch light allowed him to see my shoes. He looked down at my mismatched shoes and said, "Nice, Ruthy. Maybe it'll become the fashion. Now get in the house. Good night!"

"Good ni..."

He opened the door and shoved me inside before I could get the words out. I turned the porch light out and went straight up to my room. I threw the flip flops under the bed and sunk under my down comforter. I wondered if this whole thing was related to the first time I met Mike when he had tackled me in my front yard. It just seemed like it must have been connected, but I had no reason to think that it could be true.

Soon my mind drifted off to the usual evening thought about a certain young man with the most amazing blue eyes. Every night before I would go to sleep, I envisioned Dan's gorgeous face. I allowed myself a short daydream about what I would say the next time I saw him, and, of course, how I was going to react when he finally asked me out. Not that he ever even seemed the slightest bit interested in asking me out, but a girl can still dream. As far as I know, he had not dated any girl, and I recently started noticing that none of his friends seemed to be dating. They were always together, but it never seemed like anyone was specifically there with another person. I was too tired and did not feel like exerting the brain power needed to think about that. I would rather use the energy and enjoy my mental portrait of Dan–his blue eyes, his high cheek bones, his full lips, and his perfectly straight teeth. I missed that face today.

It was noon before I got out of bed. Sundays were usually a "special" day when Aunt Marge and Dad did something together. I enjoyed the alone time and usually used it to get the house in order, but today I was tired from a restless night. I had fallen asleep slightly after midnight, but then I woke every hour until about 6:30 a.m. when I heard Dad leave. I fell back asleep and did not wake up until noon. I know that should be enough sleep, but I am a teenager. Teenagers need more sleep than adults.

In anticipation of the little candy beggars, my dad and I had cleaned the entire house before heading to the Pumpkin Fest. That left Sunday totally as a day of rest. I went downstairs to start lunch and turned on the television. Nothing much was on. A few old movies were playing, and the weather channel was giving the prediction for the coming winter forecast. According to the forecast, I had better get a heavier coat. I flipped through a couple more channels and found a cooking show. I always feel more inspired to cook when there is a great chef on TV. She was making stuffed chicken breast with rice pilaf and an apple salad. I would be having mac-and-cheese with hotdogs, my specialty. The rest of the day moved by slowly with no unusual events. All in all, it was a boring day. I was a little surprised that Rawdy had not come over to give me the third degree about last night, but he never did. Even though there was no evidence to the contrary, I could not shake the feeling that something was wrong.

Monday morning rolled around way too early. (I cannot see how I will ever be a morning person.) I was running late, but when I got outside I noticed Rawdy's car. When he saw me, he motioned for me to get in.

"I thought you might want a ride to school today."

"Ah...thanks, Rawdy. To what do I owe this pleasure?"

"I didn't get to see you yesterday and thought it would be nice if we could talk on our way to school."

Neither of us said anything for a couple of blocks. I took the initiative and said, "So, what did you want to talk about?"

"Nothing specifically." He paused for a second then said, "Did you see Dan this weekend?"

Now that was a shocker. Surprise was written all over my face, and I could not hide it in my voice either. "Where did that question come from?"

Rawdy began stuttering, and his voice was broken and hoarse. I could not tell if he was mad or ready to cry. "No...nowhere, Ruthy. I just thought maybe you guys were getting pretty "buddy-buddy" these days, and maybe he would've said something to you or maybe one of his friends."

"What would he have said to me? How would I know what he said to one of his friends?" I was getting annoyed with the conversation. It was like he was asking me something very... specific, but at the same time he was not making any sense at all.

"Okay, Rawden Jefferson, what did you say to him?"

I was caught off guard by what I saw on his face. His face went completely white as if all the blood had drained out of it. He looked upset–scared, not mad, yet not scared of me. As his color started to come back, I noticed how horrible he looked. There were dark circles under his eyes, and they were blood shot like he had not slept in days.

"What is wrong with you, Rawdy? What's going on here?"

Rawdy pulled the car over by the side of the road. He rested his head forward on the steering wheel. I did not push him to answer me right away. I just waited for him to catch his breath. When he finally did answer, his answer was short but highly charged. "Ruthy, something happened Saturday night..." He turned and looked straight at me and tried to continue saying, "I...I...I don't know but I...I think..." He was crying.

Rawdy was not able to finish what he was saying because right then Mike opened my door and sarcastically said, "Hey, Ruthy, you wanted to get some exercise today, didn't you?" Mike was pulling me out of the car as he finished his sentence.

I was trying to protest being ripped out of the car, but I was no match for Mike. It all happened so fast that I was not able to say anything more than, "Hey!"

"Mike, man, easy on the baby Ruth." I was not sure who the guy was that said that, but his voice sounded vaguely familiar. He was standing by the rear door on the driver's side.

Rawdy just sat there watching the entire event. Why did he not help me? Why had he not stuck up for me? They both jumped in the car, and I could hear Mike tell Rawdy, "What are you waiting for, man? Get going!"

I was only a couple blocks from school, so I started walking. My mind was full of questions. It had been a strange start to the day, but more than anything I was worried about Rawdy. I had never seen him look like that before, and what did Dan have to do with any of it?

I started walking and replayed the recent event in my memory. Maybe I could figure out what was going on. "Baby Ruth!" I said under my breath with a hint of disgust–as if I have not heard that one before.

Everything appeared normal at school. I barely made it to class before the tardy bell rang, thanks to the guys. Mr. Caldwell was sitting on the edge of his desk, applying his usual nasal treatment of Vaseline. Some people never learn.

The day was going slow, but I tried to focus on each class knowing that the first chance I would get to talk to anyone would be during lunch. When I entered the cafeteria, I headed to my usual table, but only Sarah was sitting there. I went straight to her and quickly sat down.

"So, Sarah, what is going on?"

"Whatever do you mean, Ruthy?" She had a smug look on her face with the biggest smile.

"Don't play coy with me. I mean, what is that look on your face, and what do you know that I don't?" I was starting to get frustrated with all the secrets going on around me, and for some strange reason I felt like I was a part of all of them, but just did not know how, or what had involved me.

Sarah leaned across the table and whispered, "Well, don't get me wrong, Ruthy. I would love to tell you all about it, but Dan made me promise not to tell you. He wants to be the one to explain." Sarah looked around the room and quietly whispered, "He thinks if you see him before you hear the story that maybe you won't get too mad at Rawdy." As she mentioned Rawdy's name, her face went from smug to fear.

"Rawdy! What did Rawdy do to Dan?" Rising from my chair, my voice was getting louder as I talked, and Sarah was getting more embarrassed. People were starting to stare.

"Ruthy, sit down and please lower your voice!" Sarah took hold of my arm and tried to get me back in my seat. I was more successful with my protest to Sarah's actions than I had been with Mike's. I glanced around the room and noticed everyone was staring–embarrassment got the best of me. I sat down.

Just then I saw Rawdy and his two buddies standing in the doorway of the cafeteria. They were staring at me. They must have heard me, and they were headed my direction.

Sarah pleaded with me, "Ruthy, please don't tell Rawdy or Dan that I was the one who told you."

I was only halfway listening to Sarah and replied, "Huh...oh yeah, don't worry...you never said a thing." Which was absolutely the truth, all she had done was confuse me even more.

The intensity in their eyes and their size was enough to put fear in me. My heart started racing. I was not afraid of Rawdy, but there was something in his eyes that let me know he was not his usual self. I had seen a look very similar to his just a month ago. It was like his eyes were glazed over, and there was darkness behind them. I heard once that the eyes are the window to one's soul, and if that is the case, Rawdy's soul was very dark right then. My throat was extremely dry, and I could hear my heart drumming in my head. I was still mad at Rawdy, but that feeling was pushed to the side by an overwhelming desire to run and hide. I noticed that everyone in the cafeteria was making a path for the guys–like the parting of the Red Sea.

"Ruthy!" Mike growled.

"Mike, she's my family; let me talk to her...alone." Rawdy was holding out his arms in front of Mike and the other guy as if he were holding them back. They both nodded their heads and went to sit at another table. "Sarah, would you please sit somewhere else so I can talk with Ruth?"

Sarah did not say anything as she picked up her tray and moved to another table. She still had that strange look on her face–it definitely was not fear. I wondered if she had picked up on the subtle use of my proper name.

"Okay, I don't mind if you run everyone else off, but I promised Dan I would save him a seat at lunch. He told me Friday that he'd be late, but he promised he would be back by lunch."

Rawdy's face changed from anger and darkness to sadness and pity–was it for me? Before he could say anything, I spoke, "What did you say or do to Dan?"

He was still having trouble forming sentences when he said, "I...I...I really didn't *do* anything, and I certainly didn't say anything."

"Well, if you didn't *do* anything, then who did?"

"Mike didn't mean for it to happen."

"Mike! What did Mike do?" I was yelling, and again rising from my seat.

"Ruthy, please sit down and try to keep your voice down. Please!" Rawdy had his hand on my forearm, pulling me back into my seat. His eyes were racing back and forth over the crowd of gawking faces. I looked into his eyes and could see his emotions had completely changed. He was now scared and deeply sorrowful. "I am so sorry, Ruthy!" His pity was intended for me, but why?

Tears began to well up in my eyes. I tried to compose myself–it is very difficult for me to see someone else cry and not join them. I was able to lower my voice and speak more calmly. "Rawdy, please tell me what happened."

Before Rawdy could explain anything to me, Mike shouted from across the room, "A ghost!"

I looked up just in time to see Mike and his buddy running out of the cafeteria's side door. I was very shocked when I saw what they were running from. It was only Dan.

Rawdy was frozen in his chair, and his face had gone back to that bloodless white color he had been earlier that morning. He seemed to be trying to say something, but he was difficult to understand. Dan started walking over to us, and the closer he got the more frantic Rawdy became. It was as if his hands and body were glued to his chair, but his feet were trying to push him away from the table–and Dan. His chair bumped into the next table, and Rawdy shot straight up, right out of his chair.

"Rawdy, what is *wrong* with you?" I said, trying not to laugh.

"Ga...Ga...Ghost!" he finally spit out. His eyes were bulging so much they looked as if they were about to pop out of their sockets.

Dan started laughing with me. He put one hand on his hip and the other around my shoulder saying, "Ruthy, I believe your cousin here...thinks I'm dead."

Instantly I sobered up and said, "What? Somebody better start explaining to me, and I mean right now."

But once again, before anyone could say anything, we were interrupted. The principal escorted us to his office.

Mr. Douglas had taken Dan in first to get his side of the story, so while he was out of the room I quietly asked Rawdy, "Really, you thought he was a ghost? Seriously?"

"You don't understand, Ruthy. I saw him die. I held his lifeless body and had his blood on my hands. I saw the bat hit his head and..."

"What? You...hit him with a bat!"

"No, Ruthy, I didn't hit him."

"Well, who did?" I shouted.

"Ruthy, please keep your voice down, or we'll all be in much deeper trouble than we already are!"

Just then the door opened, and Mr. Douglas exchanged Dan for Rawdy.

"It'll all be ok, Ruthy. You won't have to say anything to Mr. Douglas. I explained everything. I told him you weren't involved." Dan sat down beside me and was looking straight ahead, but a full smile filled his face, and his voice was completely reassuring.

"Are you ok, Dan?" Everything Rawdy had just said began to sink in, and I was fighting back tears.

"I'm fine. Look at me, Ruthy, and you will see there are no scratches, no bruises, not even a cut. I'm fine."

"What happened to you? Rawdy said he saw you get hit in the head with a bat. How are you still alive?"

"Ruthy, right now is not the time to get into this conversation, but I promise that I'll explain it all to you as soon as I can. It's not a quaint little story. Plus, I think Rawdy needs to hear me explain it too."

"You promise?"

He turned his body toward me and grabbed both of my hands. "Ruthy, I care for you, and I want you to understand. I want you to know you are not alone."

Before I could respond, the door opened, and Mr. Douglas called me into his office. Why does it seem that every time things start to get interesting, someone interrupts?

"Ruthy, you don't have to say anything. Dan smoothed things over for both of us, and Mr. D doesn't think you were involved." Rawdy was quickly explaining the situation to me as we passed in the doorway.

As soon as school dismissed, Rawdy, Dan, and Sarah were waiting for me at the front door. Dan offered to drive us all to the park so he could talk. I was shocked when Sarah got in the car with us, but that was the least of my concerns.

The park was only a mile away, but it seemed much farther. The silence in the car was deafening, and the anguish and confusion on Rawdy's face was driving me crazy. I knew Dan was okay, so I was not really worried about him any more, and I surmised it had only been a physical altercation. Dan was not dead, so obviously Rawdy was mistaken, and maybe it was all a big joke. I could have believed that–if Rawdy had not look like he was about to vomit.

We got out of the car and went to a picnic table. They were all just standing there not saying a word, so I decided I better get things going before something or someone interrupts again, and I had to go another day without answers.

"So, who's going to start this story?"

At my cue, Dan said, "I think I better go first. Rawdy looks like he needs some relief."

Dan started explaining in great detail how he had actually died Saturday night, but was now completely fine, and Rawdy was not in any trouble. It was obvious those were the two things that had been bothering Rawdy the most–at least one of them was. He was going crazy trying to understand how Dan could be alive after being hit in such a way. He was also terrified that he had been involved in a murder, which would lead to him missing his final homecoming game (he is a linebacker). Oh, yeah, and let us not forget *prison*!

Dan began the story saying, "Every year my friends and I go on a prayer walk around town the night of the Pumpkin Fest. A prayer walk is simply where we walk around town and ask God to open the understanding of the people in every home, so they will see and understand the Truth."

Dan slid his hand down the table's edge until it was resting on top of my hand, and that is where he left it until he was done with the story.

"We were just about to end the prayer walk when I passed by your street and saw Rawdy, Mike, and Chad going door to door."

So, Chad is the name of the other guy with Rawdy and Mike. I filed his name away for future reference.

"I thought this was my chance to step up and tell them about Jesus. The whole group was with me at that point, all seven of us, and we had the Word of God with us, reading portions to them. We were trying to tell them about the love of God and His hope for their lives. Chad seemed to be the least interested in listening, but that is beside the point right now. After talking with them for about five minutes, Mike said he was done with it, and he needed to catch a couple more houses before 9:30. Chad followed, and as you know, Rawdy, you soon left too.

"I thought we had really touched you with a few things we said, and I didn't feel like we were done, but our youth leader said it was getting late, and we needed to head back in the direction of our cars. We all started heading back when I heard something being pulverized, and then I heard a couple of loud voices. We'd just passed two young boys who were out collecting candy without their parents. I was concerned they might be hurt or had stumbled across Chad's path. You know his temper, Rawdy, but the young boys were nowhere around, it was only Chad and Mike. At least that's all I could see.

"I started walking up to Chad, but before I could say anything, he swung the bat and hit me in the chest. It knocked the air right out of me, and I fell to the ground. Mike came running over and helped me up. I was back on my feet when Chad swung the bat at my head. I couldn't see straight, and all I could hear was a ringing. Then I didn't feel anything. I didn't feel the last blow, striking me square between my shoulder blades. Down I went, and I was dead." Dan was silent for a few seconds, and then he started talking again.

"The rest of the story was told to me by other members of the FFJ's. Sarah noticed that I was not with them when they got to the cars; she informed the others, and they all went looking for me. When they found my body, it was ice cold; there was blue under my finger nails and on my lips. They felt for a pulse, but there wasn't one. A couple of the guys started CPR, but it was too late. There was a huge pool of blood from my head wound. They said that the whole left side of my skull was smashed in."

At that description, Rawdy's entire body shivered; I assumed he was reliving the memory. It was at that point I realized why Sarah was there. I had assumed that Dan had asked her to come to bridge the gap between him and Rawdy, or at least to give her account of the story, but that was not the case. Sarah never intended to give an account, and Dan seemed as shocked as I was to see her getting into his car. She was not going to say anything, and Dan had never intended for her to be at the meeting. Rawdy must have invited her to come; she was someone that he trusted, and yet he knew she was also an FFJ. When Rawdy's body shivered, Sarah reached out for him, putting her arms around his, resting her head on his back.

Dan continued, "They knew I was dead, but these are people of faith and they were not going to believe what science would say. Science would say I was a lost cause. My brain had been without oxygen for too long, my brain matter was oozing out of my head, and there is no way that I could come back from that much blood loss. My friends, on the other hand, had read stories of people coming back to life, and they knew there's a power stronger than any science book has taught–the power of God. My friends started speaking the words from God and asking God to heal me–they didn't stop for an hour, but nothing changed, and I still looked the same. That's when Sarah laid herself down across my body three times and started crying out to God in a loud voice, 'Heavenly Father, let this boy's life return to him!' and then it happened."

Rawdy snapped around releasing himself from Sarah's hold. He was obviously not comfortable hearing her role in the story. Her face went from concern to rejection, then sorrow.

Dan did not seem to notice, and just continued telling the story.

"I gasped for air, and in the time it takes to blink, my body was totally restored like new. My hair had blood in it, but my head wasn't smashed in anymore, my ribs were no longer broken, nor was my left arm, and I could see and hear clearly. My clothes were a mess, but all of that we could fix. Chris, my youth leader, made me go to the hospital and get checked out, just to be on the safe side—only after I had a shower and changed clothes. None of us wanted anyone getting in trouble for this. We were trying to save souls, not condemn them to prison, and with me alive there was no proof or reason for anyone else to suffer. I spent most of Sunday being poked and prodded at the hospital, but I checked out perfect. There was one strange thing the doctor found. He had a bunch of x-rays taken, and even though I currently had no broken bones, he could see that, at one time, I had several major breaks, but everything had healed quite well. I had to run a couple of errands this morning, that's why I was late to school, and lunch was the first time I had a chance to talk to either of you. I never meant to scare you guys like that, but I didn't know the proper way to inform you that I was no longer dead. So, that's my story. Do you have anything you want to add?" Dan looked at Sarah and Rawdy.

Sarah was not in the least bit interested in adding anything to the story, and Rawdy still looked a little dazed.

So Dan added, "Ruthy, I'm very sorry I didn't say something to you sooner about the prayer walk. I knew in the car, that first day, you needed answers, and I've held back from telling you some things. Sometimes our own desires scream at us louder than the Holy Spirit speaks to us."

Just then, Rawdy started talking, "We had almost filled our pillow sacks when your little group of freaks walked up to us and started talking about Jesus. None of us really cared to listen, but you were pretty persistent. You guys finally left, and Chad was pretty ticked off.

"We had a plan to get back at this old lady on Ruthy's street." Rawdy looked at me and explained, "That's why Mike had the baseball bat. Every year Ms. Beverly Mae gets up in our business and tells us we are too old to be dressed up and asking for candy. She doesn't know how hard we work to harvest those pumpkins and help farmer Findlay prepare for the festival. Is it too much to ask for a little fun in return? Four years ago Mike started smashing her pumpkins after the festival. I know it's childish, but everyone just throws them away the next day anyway. This was the last year we were going to dress up, and Mike had been planning this night all year. Ms. Beverly Mae had bought a security camera last year, and Mike was trying to make sure none of us got caught."

I interrupted, "Is that the little old lady that lives three houses down from me?"

"Yeah, anyway, we got to her house, and Mike smashed her pumpkins, but I was still bothered by our encounter with Dan's group, and Chad was still ticked off. The next thing I knew, Chad was going down the street hitting every pumpkin. He even started down another street. Mike went after Chad. That's when I heard Dan scream from pain. By the time I got to the guys, Dan had already been hit twice. I stepped forward trying to stop Chad, but he let loose and hit Dan square between the shoulder blades. I heard his arm break, and he fell into my arms. Dude, your head hit my chest, and we both fell to the ground. You weren't moving or breathing, and there was so much blood. I couldn't feel a pulse. Chad and Mike tried to get me to leave, but I couldn't, at least not until Sarah came around the corner. She got to me before any of your other friends. She told me to run. Sarah was very calm and assured me you would be okay." Rawdy looked straight at Sarah and said, "You never called me Sunday. I thought you would call. I was going crazy over the whole deal." Sarah did not respond, instead she tried to touch his arm, but Rawdy would not allow it.

Rawdy continued saying, "I spent the whole day trying to get your blood off of me and my clothes. I felt so bad for Ruthy because I knew she cared about you, and if I had just let you die... well, it wasn't something she needed to go through this year. I went to her house this morning to pick her up and to explain, but I didn't have the words to explain. Mike and Chad found us and threw her out of the car. Then I heard them scream, 'Ghost!', at lunch and saw you standing in the cafeteria. End of story."

There was an extended period of silence.

"Rawdy, I forgive you," Dan said with complete sincerity.

"Well, Dan, I don't think I deserve your forgiveness. I didn't hit you with the bat, but I didn't stop Chad either, man...I just left you."

Sarah was the one to interrupt this time saying, "Rawdy, I made you leave because I knew you couldn't do anything more at that point, but we could."

Rawdy threw his hands up and said, "This is all just a little too much for me to handle right now. I'm glad you're alive, Dan, and I'm thankful to you, Sarah, for trying to protect me, but this all just creeps me out. For crying out loud, he was dead! Doesn't that seem a little strange to you, Ruthy?"

"Rawdy, there are ideas and beliefs you have taken as fact over the years that I now know are not true, and the fact that Dan was dead but is now alive is just one of many. Please, Rawdy, listen to Dan, let him explain the Truth to you." I could hear Rawdy's thoughts, and he was scared, but he was even angrier with me for caring about Sarah and Dan. I took a step behind Dan for protection. It was the first time in my life that I ever felt scared of Rawdy, even the time he locked me in the shed for hours when I was eleven did not scare me as bad.

Rawdy eyed me as I slipped behind Dan; he had his fill of our conversation and was not going to listen to any of us. He bolted off running down the road. Sarah started to run after him, but there was no way she could catch him. She had only made it a few yards before she resolved herself to defeat. I could not believe that I had misread her affection for him, but it was obvious now that she cared very deeply for him, and I suspected that he felt the same for her.

Dan put his arm around me and once again said, "Ruthy, I'm so sorry I didn't tell you sooner."

I just laughed and said, "You were actually dead, and you're saying you're sorry for not telling me about your prayer walk. Do you honestly…understand how much it would have devastated me if you had died…forever?"

"I didn't just know about the prayer walk. I knew something was going to happen, and I didn't warn you. I didn't spare you the heartache of this day."

"What? What are you saying? You knew you were going to die?"

Dan looked over to where Sarah was standing, sadness filled his eyes, and then he said, "I think Sarah needs to get home. We can drop her off, and then I'll explain. I'd also like to talk about this mind thing of yours."

6

My Thoughts; Your Thoughts

Monday was a school night, and I knew my dad would have a problem with me being out late, so I suggested we go to my house and talk. When we got to my house, I went in to tell Dad we would be out on the swing, but he interrupted and told me to invite Dan in to eat with us. It was obvious that my dad was not going to let me get away with not eating, and I knew Dan must be getting hungry too. So our talk would have to wait at least another half hour.

Dad is an amazing cook, and had prepared a delectable meal of garlic chicken and sundried tomatoes with pasta. It was a complete meal in itself and one of my favorites. Dad told us his little secret of using pasta water to hydrate the sundried tomatoes instead of just tap water. It was something about the starch in the pasta water, and he said you never add oil to your pasta or run cold water over it. Once again, that had something to do with the starch of the pasta and the sauce. Dad was a chef in his early twenties, and every chance he got he tried to teach me the finer points of cooking. I always reminded him that I was a baker, not a chef. The half hour meal turned into forty-five minutes due to Dan's immense appetite. He had two helpings of pasta and three pieces of apple pie. I had made the pie and found a simple pleasure in Dan's enjoyment of my creation.

Dan was obviously stuffed. He complemented my dad by saying, "Sir, thank you so much for a wonderful meal. I'm so full I could fall asleep right here."

I grabbed his arm and tried to pull him up from his chair while exclaiming, "Oh...no you don't! You came over to talk with me, and you are not going to put this off another day."

I had forgotten my dad was oblivious to the other side of my life. His expression was clear that he was not pleased with my attitude or my tone of voice. My dad was not going to let it go without a few words. "Ruth Ann, I didn't raise you to be rude. You'll apologize to Dan this instant. I'm so sorry for her lack of manners, Dan."

I was embarrassed and angry, but I knew that I could not explain my actions without complicating things, so I resolved myself to apologize. "I am very sorry, Dan, for the rude way that I spoke to you and for trying to pull you out of the chair before you were ready. Will you sit on the porch swing with me and talk for a while?" I thought that would satisfy my dad, but I was wrong.

Dan started to stand up and say something, but Dad stopped him and said, "It's Monday night, Ruthy, and I'm sure Dan would rather sit and watch the game." Dad turned toward Dan and said, "Dan, would you like to watch the game with us?"

I turned red in the face and thought I might say something inappropriate. I had waited all through dinner and the drive when we dropped Sarah off, just for the chance to talk to Dan and find out about *the mind thing*. The game would last until ten o'clock, and then my dad would expect Dan to leave, and me to go to bed. Dan is a complete gentleman, so I knew he would not want to offend my dad, but he had also promised me. He would not go back on his word. Would he? Honestly, I did not know what he was going to do.

"Sir, I would love to watch the game with you, but I missed today's morning classes, and I really need a chance to talk with Ruthy. Could I get a rain check on the game...say next Monday?"

My dad looked pleased that Dan would want to reschedule. "Sure...sure that will be no problem. You kids go get caught up. I'll make my famous salmon steaks for you next week."

"That sounds great, sir."

"Ruthy, you should probably take a blanket."

"I will, Dad."

I was not sure how he did it, but Dan had satisfied my dad, and, at the same time, kept his promise to me–Dad was even making his specialty dish for him. Dan had not lied about missing school, and he did not say that we were going to talk about homework. So, he had not stretched the truth. And to top it all off, he was even willing to sacrifice next week's Monday evening to watch football with my dad. Well, I could see how the last part was not much of a sacrifice, in the fact that Dan loved to watch sports, and he loved my dad's cooking, but it was still going to be my father, not "the guys".

I picked up the fleece blanket, and we walked to the swing. Dan took the blanket from me and motioned for me to sit down. I obligingly complied. He followed me and gently whipped the blanket up in the air letting it fall over our legs. Everything Dan did was graceful and majestic. He put his right arm around my shoulders and held my left hand. Then he looked straight at me and said, "What did I miss at school this morning?"

I wrinkled my nose and turned up the left corner of my mouth. "What?"

He laughed at the face I was making and tried to imitate me. "I told your dad that I'd missed some classes this morning, and I want to be totally honest. So, tell me what I missed."

"You are actually going to make me talk about this, aren't you? I should have known."

I spent the next ten minutes telling him minuscule details of each class. I was also able to give him a short story about his friend Caleb. "We had a locker check at school today."

"What were they looking for?" He seemed genuinely concerned.

"Only in a small town could a story like this ever exist. In large city schools they have locker checks for drugs, alcohol, and maybe even firearms."

"Whose locker was checked?"

"Well, in the end all our lockers were checked, but it was started by your friend Caleb."

"Caleb? He's even more straight laced than I am."

"Yeah, I know. I thought it was pretty outrageous that they would blame Caleb for anything, but he had done it."

"Done what? What was in his locker, Ruthy?"

I started to giggle and said, "A glass soda bottle."

"What? A glass soda bottle?!"

"Only in a small school would they have locker checks for glass soda bottles. Caleb brought two sodas to school and gave one to Josh and kept the other one. Josh had been drinking out of his between classes, and after third hour he dropped it. It was like a fountain spewing soda all over the ceiling, walls, and the floor. Josh took full responsibility for it, but when they wanted to search everyone's locker, Caleb stepped up and said he brought the sodas, and he had another one in his locker."

"Wow! That would've been something to see the soda exploding!"

"Okay, enough of this. Are you ready to talk?"

Dan was obviously tired and could easily fall asleep at any moment, but he was going to keep his word. He removed his arm from around me and took my left hand in his right hand. His hand was cold, so I tucked both of our hands under the blanket.

"First, I want to know what happened to Caleb and Josh."

"Well, Josh had to clean it all up, and they both got in-school suspension for a day."

"I am sorry, Ruthy, but I'm a little more tired that I thought. My brain isn't working quite right. Could you maybe ask me a question to get me thinking in the right direction?"

"Dan, I hate seeing you this tired. Do you need to go home? We can talk about this tomorrow night."

As much as I hated to wait another minute to have this conversation, I cared about Dan, and it was hurting me to see him so miserably tired.

"No, I'll be fine. Maybe we can just talk about this for an hour and then call it a night. Would that be ok?"

"Yeah, that's fine with me if you can stay awake that long."

"I made you a promise, Ruthy, and I want to keep it."

Just then my dad came outside with two cups of hot cocoa. "I can't believe you two are still sitting out here. I won't ask you to leave, Dan, or ask you to come inside, Ruthy, but it is a school night, and I would like you to be in the house by ten o'clock. That's in an hour."

Dan stood up to help my dad through the door and took his cup of hot cocoa. "Thank you, sir. This really hits the spot. Ruthy will be in the house by ten, I promise."

"Thank you."

"Thanks, Dad." I grabbed my cup off of the tray, never moving from my spot on the swing.

Dad turned around and walked back into the house. I wondered if he had seen us holding hands, or if Dan had let go before he could see. Dan came back to the swing, and we were both holding our cups, trying to sip the hot, molten lava. Dad has had this idea that if something was not scalding hot then it was luke-warm and only worth being spit out. We did not talk for a couple of minutes, and I almost came to the conclusion that this was not going to be the night for our talk, but just when I was ready to give up all hope, Dan started talking.

"Ruthy, what I wanted to explain before is not a simple concept. Some churches have a different understanding than others. So what I am going to tell you is what I have experienced, and what my church has come to believe."

"Ok. I know you are only seventeen, so I don't expect you to be an expert." I wanted him to hurry up and spit it out, but it was obvious that he was taking this very serious.

"Ruthy, you told me that you belonged to the Azusa Gathering in California for a few weeks. I don't know how much, if anything, they taught you about the giftings God gives us, or how God equips His people. Usually we start out by teaching new believers about God's grace, mercy, love, and about Jesus and His disciples. This often takes a few months to a year. Then after they have a grasp of the basics of God, we start teaching them about being chosen of God. We are the chosen ones, Ruthy."

I had never heard the things Dan was explaining–he had my full attention.

"You said you knew the thoughts of that boy Jacob, and you knew he had a gun."

"Yeah, that's right."

"Well, you are a chosen one; every believer is a chosen one. Ruthy, have you ever heard any of this before?"

"No, but the group I was with did teach me about Jesus, and how He died for all of us, but few people are willing to make Him their Lord and Savior. Is that what makes us chosen ones?"

"Yes, plus we have all received the Holy Spirit with power and fire. Jesus said that when He left, He would send the Comforter, which is the Holy Spirit. We are made whole, or complete, through the Holy Spirit." Dan sat both of our cocoas down and took my hands. His eyes were so heavy, but they were filled with immense love and tenderness. "Ruthy, you can't read minds."

"I can't?" My gaze was cut off by his words, and I looked to the floor.

"We don't read other people's minds, but God does tell us things. If you could read minds then you would have known that Jacob was going to kill himself, and you wouldn't have stopped until someone listened to you. I know you, Ruthy! You knew he had a gun, and that there was danger in store for Jacob and maybe others."

"Yes...I guess you're right. I didn't know everything he was thinking. I even tried to hear more of what he was thinking, but never got anything."

"You were never hearing him think; you just knew a few of his thoughts. Did you ever stop and think of how many lives you might have saved that day just because you went to school? So, I'm definitely not saying God made you sick, but a normal kid would have stayed at home as sick as you were, yet you were compelled by something to go that day. Weren't you?"

"Yes, I was. I remember waking up that morning feeling cold and could hardly speak, but I knew I had to go to school, and yet the only thing I really wanted to do was go sing my song and get my 'I+'. I can't explain why, but I had to go to school that day."

"And that statement, right there, is what makes you a chosen one. As a chosen one, we live our life to please the Lord, and we try to do His will and desire instead of living for our own human desires and comforts. God doesn't make us do anything, we have a free will, but He will show us, or should I say, guide us on the journey of our life. The hard part is that there is an evil one who tries to seduce us and tempt us, but God, on the other hand, is like a still small voice, and there is no seduction with God. So many people are accustomed to being led by their lusts that it is hard for them to follow God."

"So what does this have to do with minds?"

"Well, it's all very much connected. You were trying to live your life for God, yet you still have desires of your human nature. You and others at Bayside High were in danger, so God used you to save the students."

"Why did He let Jacob kill himself?"

"Back to what I said before, God gave us a free will, and He isn't going to take that away from us. God gave Jacob another chance when you confronted him about his gun. It made Jacob think, and he did change his mind. But Jacob had been living his life fulfilling all of his human desires, and the pull of anger and revenge was just too strong in the end."

"Oh...so, do you hear thoughts? Do you hear my thoughts?"

Dan started laughing and said, "Well, I don't know if you understand yet or not. Neither you nor I actually hear people's thoughts. We hear from God. It's kind of like a radio station with one channel, but unless you tune into it, you can only hear static... basically you hear nothing. When you become a believer and receive the Holy Spirit, who is also known as the Comforter, then you're tuned into that one station, and God gives us direction through that signal. But we need to know the words from God, and we must "practice" listening to His voice. Otherwise, we'll get interference from other sources."

He definitely lost me with that analogy, and I knew he could see it on my face, so I just exclaimed, "Huh?"

"We, FFJ's, do not read minds, but God speaks to us and tells us things. Does that make sense?"

"Yeah, I guess so. So I didn't read Jacob's mind?"

"No! You can't read minds."

"Don't get so huffy. I was just saying it out loud. I think I get it now. I was hearing God's mind, or heart, or something."

"Yes, you could say it that way. I guess I should've thought of that sooner. You have to give me some slack. I'm exhausted, and my brain is not working at full speed right now."

"Well, it could've been due to that nasty hit on the head you took Saturday night." I started laughing as I finished my statement.

Dan took his right hand away and tapped me on the shoulder. "Hey!"

"So, you're telling me that God told you that you would be killed Saturday night?"

"Wow, your brain is still fully functioning. No, He didn't really tell me that. You know how you were compelled to go to school the day Jacob killed himself?"

"Yeah."

"Well, I was compelled to pursue Chad. And Friday God told me that I was going to be in danger, but that everything would be alright in the end. I also knew that I was going to miss the quiz in second hour on Monday. That's why, on Friday, I skipped the rally and took the quiz early. If you remember, we were never told before hand that we'd be having a quiz on Monday. I went to Ms. Andrews and told her I was going to miss her class Monday, and I really didn't want to lose any credits. So she told me she was going to give a quiz, and if I promised not to tell anyone or share the questions, then she would allow me to take the quiz early."

"So, what were you doing Monday morning that caused you to miss your classes? You said you were in the hospital Sunday but didn't stay the night."

"Well, I had to report to the leadership council of our church. Any time a miracle such as someone being raised from the dead occurs, they want a full report on the incident."

"Oh…so tell me if I have this right. We don't really know all the facts, but, when something major is going to happen, God gives us a heads up. Is that it?"

"Well, it is not always major things. Sometimes it's a simple answer to another believer's request, or sometimes God wants to tell us something, and it's not always a thought that pops into your head. God gives us dreams, visions, and He does audibly speak too."

"Really? That is amazing! So...what about you coming back to life? I know I've heard stories about that in God's Word, but how did Sarah do that?"

"Well, I wouldn't say it was just because of Sarah, but God did use her. She was given a gift of faith for my healing and was compelled to lay her body across mine and proclaim the words from God. Just as you and I have been compelled, she was compelled, but the rest of my group had faith and was asking God to heal me as a sign to Rawdy, Chad, and Mike. God listened."

"So, God let you know you were in danger but would be ok in the end. Are you telling me God made all this happen to you?"

"No, it wasn't God's plan or God's desire for me to be beaten and killed. Once again, Chad is led by his human desires, and anger and rage took him over. I will say that God warned me there would be danger, but if I trusted Him, I would be okay. I could have stayed away from the guys that night, and I still believe God would be okay with that, but my desire in life is to help others see what a wonderful God we serve. If I hadn't gone that night, Rawdy wouldn't be contemplating his beliefs right now. Mike and Chad are scared, but I still have hope they'll come around. Oh, by the way, do you know Mike likes you?"

"What? Did you hear that thought?"

"No, I didn't need to hear that thought. I could see it written all over his face. Plus, he told Emma, who told Nancy, who in turn told Sarah, who told me."

"Well, you don't have anything to worry about. I am not in the least bit interested in him."

"Oh, I know that." He had a smirk on his face as he answered.

"Back to the topic at hand, are there other *powers* that we have?"

"You might call them powers, if you like. Basically, the fastest way to explain this would be to say that, anything miraculous that happened in God's Word can still happen today. It can happen to, and through, us."

"Really! That is most interesting!"

Dan was starting to yawn, and I knew it was almost ten, so I resigned myself to the fact that the rest of my questions would have to wait.

"Dan, you need to get going. It's late and Dad will be out to get me soon. I want you to be able to keep your word and have me back in my house before ten o'clock."

It was obvious that Dan agreed, and as he stood up folding the blanket, I got out of the swing. He handed me the blanket and started to walk to his car. "Oh, Ruthy, you need to come to my church. We meet every Thursday night at six-thirty sharp. Do you want me to pick you up?"

"Yes, thank you for the invitation; I'd love to go."

"Ok...well...I'll see you tomorrow."

"Good night." Dan was in his car and driving away before I got into the house. I knew he must have been exhausted because as a rule he would never have left me outside on the porch. He is such a gentleman that he normally would have insisted upon me entering my house before he stepped off the porch. I turned to open the door and almost jumped out of my shoes. Dad was standing at the door watching me. So, that is why Dan did not walk me to the door; he must have seen my dad standing there. "So, Dad, what were you watching?"

"I just wanted to see how true to his word that boy would be. He left you three minutes before you were supposed to be in this house, and I must say I'm very impressed with him. Rawdy had warned me, but I think he was overreacting."

"Rawdy did what?" I was furious! Not only had Dad been testing Dan, Rawdy had also warned my dad about him.

"Ruthy...honey...Rawdy is just concerned for you. He told me last week that Dan wasn't good enough for you, but from what I saw of that young man tonight, I think he is overqualified." He started laughing.

"So, you like Dan?"

"Yes, honey...very much. I don't mind if you bring him over, but I don't want this to affect your grades."

"No problem, Dad. Hey, Dad?"

"Yeah, Ruthy."

"I love you."

He stepped closer to me and gave me a hug and a kiss on the top of my head. "I love you too, kiddo."

I went up to bed, not fully convinced it was possible for me to fall asleep after the day I had just lived. The guy I liked had actually been dead and came back to life, coupled with the explanation about not reading minds and having powers; it was almost more than I could bear...for one day.

My anticipation was growing for Thursday night's meeting. It would be beneficial to acquire training for the powers Dan spoke of, plus, it would give me another reason to spend time with him.

I was startled by my alarm going off; it was already six o'clock Tuesday morning. I jumped out of bed and got ready for school, but before I could get downstairs, the doorbell rang. Would Dan have come to drive me to school? He never mentioned anything the night before, and Dan was usually not the spontaneous type.

Before I could see who was at the door, I heard my dad say, "Good morning, Rawdy."

7

Friend or Foe

"Hey, Ruthy, how are you?" Rawdy looked like a mess, and his voice was raspy.

"I'm good, Rawdy, and you?" I was trying to keep the conversation light hearted. He had totally caught me off guard. I was not expecting Rawdy. And my dad was standing beside him, watching our interaction. I did not want to initiate any in-depth discussion.

"I need some more sleep, besides that I'm fine. Ah…would you like a ride to school today?" He said it more as a command than a question, while he was gesturing we should leave, pointing with his hands at the door.

"Are Mike and Chad going to ride with us today?"

"No, they're not. So will you? Hope you don't mind, but I need a coffee. Do you mind if we run by the Coffee Hut first?"

"No, I don't mind…it beats walking. I could use a coffee-vanilla bean spin myself." I mentioned walking for my dad's benefit. I had been asking for a car for over a year. But he was against me driving in California, and so far had not given me as much as a hint if he considered driving in a small town more permissible than in a large city.

Rawdy and I walked to his car without exchanging a single word. He was still wearing the clothes from yesterday; unfortunately, I was also close enough to smell his breath and could tell he had not brushed his teeth either. Once again it was obvious he had not gotten much sleep. We got to his car, and he opened my door. That was a huge surprise, but I glanced over my shoulder and noticed my dad standing on the porch. Apparently I was not the only one to notice Rawdy's lack of hygiene and sleep deprivation. It made complete sense that Rawdy was only opening my door for my dad's benefit–a feeble attempt to show some form of civility. After all, I was his cousin, not a date. He slid into the driver's seat and abruptly said, "Put on your seat belt...please."

The way he said it made it sound like a command not a request. I had expected that this encounter could be a scary event, but I was not prepared enough for this. My mind was racing with scenarios. Had Chad and Mike convinced him that he needed to set things right? Was he really that mad about the FFJ thing? In the back of my mind I even wondered if he could be jealous of my relationship with Dan. Not that Rawdy wanted to be my boyfriend, but Dan and I were becoming best friends and sharing things that I would have told Rawdy in the past. Plus, with Dan and I both being FFJ's, it put Rawdy on the outside.

I tried to stop my incessant imagination. My face was hot, obviously red, and I could hear my heartbeat in my head. Even breathing was becoming more labored and the monster blackness was closing in on me. It was growing impossible for me to stop yawning, and there were only two small white dots of light that the darkness had not yet overtaken. The ringing in my ears started to get louder, and I knew it would not be long.

"Rawdy, I think I...I'm going to faint."

"No! Not in the car, Ruthy!" Panic was evident in Rawdy's tone.

Finally, I completely surrendered to the darkness. The next thing I knew, I could hear Rawdy talking, and I could feel something cool and wet under my body. There was still a slight ringing, but slowly it faded and my vision returned. I could see that I was lying on the grassy curb by Highway Eight. Rawdy was hovering over me and talking on his cell phone. I heard him say, "Oh, thank goodness, she's awake. Ok...thank you very, very much. Ruthy, can you hear me? Can you hear me, Ruthy? Speak to me, please!"

"Dude, I was just going to faint...not vomit. Why didn't you want me in your car?" My voice was a little breathy, and my eye sight was still a little fuzzy, but the episode was all but over.

"Oh, Ruthy, I'm glad you're alright. I was so worried. Don't do that to me again!" His compassion was starting to wear off when he answered my question. "Well, I didn't know if you would...you know...lose control of bodily functions."

"Oh...that's just gross! Come on, help me up, and let's get back in the car. I'm getting wet from the ground."

I reached my hands out, and Rawdy pulled me to my feet. He steadied me as I walked back to the car, then we both got in. But he just sat there, looking at me with confusion and said, "What made you faint?"

How could I answer that question? If I told him the truth he might be hurt or think I am an idiot, but what else could I say? I had never been any good at making up stories or lying–my body had a way of telling on me when I lied. I finally decided that honesty was the best policy and said, "You scared me." I kept my eyes fixed on my fingernails as I spoke, and did not even look up when I finished.

The engine started, and we were off again. He was silent for a few minutes, and then he started to speak. He was looking straight out the front windshield when he said, "I didn't mean to scare you." His voice was very soft and gentle. He spoke in low tones with no evidence of anger.

"Well, it's just that I...I didn't know how you would respond to everything yesterday, and you're not exactly acting normal. Plus, you know me, I don't just wear my heart on my sleeve, my whole body reacts to my emotions."

"It was a lot to take in at one time. I was mad at you for a while, well maybe I still am, but more than anger, I'm shocked. People are not supposed to come back to life, and I don't care what Chad says, I know that Dan was dead."

So he had talked to the guys, or at least Chad. I was still not comfortable in his presence, and part of me wanted to jump out of his car at the next stop. I was not sure why, but Rawdy was not acting like my Rawdy. He had always picked on me as a kid, but he never let anyone else hurt me. One time a bully was calling me names, and he walked right over to the kid and told him to leave me alone. The other kid threatened Rawdy, but he fired back by saying, "Give me your best shot." The kid hauled off and hit his nose and broke it. Rawdy hit him back defending my honor, but Rawdy never blamed me or complained, and he even called his broken nose a badge of courage. I wondered if he would still stand up for my honor if that were to happen today.

After a moment of reflection, I responded to his comment. "Yes, Dan did die, and I do understand that it's a lot to take in. Please understand that I hadn't heard of anything like this happening in modern day either. I was just as shocked as you, and maybe even more upset at you for not stopping Chad from hurting

Dan. Why weren't you with Chad and Mike when this was going on?"

"I already told that story."

"Why do I think you're not telling me the whole story?"

"Leave it alone, Ruthy!" His right hand was holding his face rigidly, and his eyes were intense.

"Why can't you tell me? You used to tell me everything."

"Look who's talking! You've been keeping a pretty major secret, haven't you?" He let go of his face and grabbed the steering wheel.

Rawdy was right; I had been keeping a lot of secrets from him lately.

"I guess the older you get the less black and white things seem."

"Huh? What are you talking about?"

"You and I had once promised to tell each other everything... no matter what, but things started to get complicated, and I was only trying to protect you. Then I wasn't sure how to explain, and in the end the "no matter what" promise wasn't so crucial."

"Ruthy, I just can't talk about it."

Rawdy's words ended the conversation as we pulled into the school parking lot. I noticed that Dan's assigned parking spot was empty, which was not a big surprise because we were still early. Rawdy had picked me up about fifteen minutes earlier than I usually left the house. Since I was without a car, I had been walking to school, but it was only a few blocks. Rawdy had wanted a coffee before school, so we had driven a few miles to the local coffee stand. I fainted before we got there, and after that whole episode, Rawdy decided to just forget the coffee and head to school.

As we got closer to Rawdy's parking spot, I noticed a group of people standing nearby. It was Chad, Mike, Chloe, and a couple of their friends that I did not know. I must have turned green because Rawdy looked at me and said, "Now don't you go fainting on me again." I did not respond. I was too perplexed by the whole situation to know what to think, let alone say. Was Rawdy my friend or foe?

Rawdy got out of the car first, came around to my door, and opened it for me. I was reasonably content with staying in the car and only made an effort to exit when Rawdy grabbed my elbow and pulled me out.

"Well, if it ain't little Miss *Dan* herself." Chad exclaimed with a sharp tone of sarcasm.

Mike was the next to speak. "Chad, leave her alone! Thanks for entering the three legged race with me on Saturday, Ruthy. It's too bad we lost."

It seemed like Mike was trying to be civil, and I did not see any harm in responding to his comments. "I enjoyed the race too. I'm sure we could've won if we hadn't collided with those other competitors."

"Well...I think we all know that I didn't collide with anyone." He turned his head and looked at all his friends, then continued by saying, "That's all on you, Ruthy." Mike's voice had a sharp bite to it, and it made my heart hurt. He and all of his friends, including Rawdy, were laughing at me. I wanted to run and hide because I knew, right then, something was wrong. Mike had been so insistent on me not blaming myself the day of the race, and now he was willing to put all the blame on me.

I said a quick little request under my breath, asking God to get Dan to school fast. God answered me, and in less than a minute

Dan's car was pulling into his spot. Everyone turned their head as Dan's car arrived. Chad and Mike simultaneously said, "I got to go now," and they headed for the front door. Only Rawdy was still standing by me when Dan finally reached us.

"Hey, Rawdy! How's it going?"

"Hey...Dan! I'm pretty good and you?"

"Good...good."

"Good."

There was an excruciatingly long pause until Rawdy finally said,

"Well, I better be heading in too. Do you want a ride home, Ruthy?"

Before I could answer, Dan answered for me. "Thanks, Rawdy, but Ruthy will be riding home with me."

"Okay. I'll see you later, Ruthy."

"Bye, Rawdy." I was still in shock over the whole Mike thing, and was so relieved Dan was next to me. Even though I said goodbye to Rawdy, I did not watch him leave.

Dan stood behind me, but it was not until after Rawdy entered the building that he turned me toward him and asked, "Are you okay?"

I was clearly not "okay." I had tears streaming down my face. I tried to make them stop, at least enough to talk with him. I was using the palm of my hands, fervently wiping away tears. "I'm okay now. I thank God that you showed up when you did."

"I heard God tell me that you were in...well, that you needed me." Dan interrupted himself and changed his phrasing. I was not sure if it was a mistake or for my benefit that he did so.

"I asked Him to send you."

"Ruthy, what happened? Did they hurt you?"

"No, they didn't physically hurt me, just my pride. Mike said something, and they all laughed at me, but it was as if they were laughing at me for some other reason entirely, almost like they were mad at me, or even hated me. I don't know if I can get through this day. It has already been a long day, and school hasn't even started. Rawdy picked me up this morning..."

Dan interrupted me and asked, "Why did he do that? Did he say anything specific?"

"No, he didn't say or ask me anything really. We started to talk and then I fainted and..."

"You fainted! Why?"

"Okay...if you are going to be around me you'll have to understand that I faint from time to time. It happens when I get overwhelmed. It was nothing, and I am perfectly fine now. I've had all the tests, and I am perfectly healthy. The doctors say I'm just someone who faints. Rawdy scared me...by his actions...nothing really, but as far as why he came to pick me up...I don't know why. I was starting to wonder if his little crowd was part of a plan...that is right until you drove up. They still seem scared of you." I had a smile beaming across my face when I said that last line.

Dan was very serious, and after a short pause he explained, "Ruthy, I was concerned something like this might happen, and I now believe it's imperative that you ride with Sarah to school."

"What? I am perfectly capable of walking." I could hardly believe what I was saying, but I did not want to be treated like a child, and he was forcing me to be driven to school. I would not stand for it even if it was Sarah.

"I don't want to see you get hurt. Please do this for me?"

"Why can't you pick me up?"

"That would be inappropriate. Your dad holds me to a higher standard, and I don't want to disappoint him."

I hated to admit it, but he was right. My dad would never let me ride to school with him. At least not *everyday*, and I could see by the intensity in his face that he was very serious about this issue. I resigned to the fact that I would be riding with Sarah and reluctantly let him off the hook by saying, "You're right, but will Sarah want to pick me up everyday?"

"You leave Sarah to me. Thank you, Ruthy." There was a sadness in his eyes which made me very curious as to his motives.

"What is it, Dan? Please tell me!"

He contemplated his answer for a while and then said, "I don't trust Mike or Chad, and I believe Rawdy is allowing them to influence him. I don't want you to go through what I had to go through."

"But you're alive. God totally healed you, and you look perfect, not even a scratch."

"Ruthy, you're right, I don't have any broken bones, not a single scratch, or even a bruise, but those are only outward signs of a fight. You see...Ruthy...I remember every time the bat hit me, except for the very last one. I remember the pain, and I do mean pain. It was excruciating, and then he hit me in the head, and I heard a crack that echoed over and over and over, and that's when I blacked out. I believe I was already gone by the time he hit me between the shoulders. I just hadn't fallen yet."

"I didn't realize that you could remember the pain." He had totally taken me off guard with his latest revelation. "The way you explained the story yesterday led me to believe you did not remember...the pain."

"I didn't want to hurt you–I didn't want to hurt Rawdy. I thought he might want to join us, so every word I used was chosen very carefully, all for the purpose of trying to win Rawdy to the Truth."

"You are such an amazing guy."

Dan took a hold of my face and spoke into my right ear. "Ruthy, it's hard for me to think about that pain. Then there are the dreams I have about that night, yet I can bear all of that because it was me, and I am alive, but I couldn't take it if the same thing happened to you. Please ride with Sarah and try to avoid being alone with Rawdy, at least for a while."

There was so much pain in his eyes, and all I wanted to do was make it all go away. I put my hand to his cheek, and he leaned into my hand. I felt a cool tear drop hit my thumb. Could I be as brave as him? Could I live with the memory even after the scars were gone? He was breaking my heart, and I had to give him some peace. "I'll ride with Sarah and will do my best not to be alone with Rawdy or any of his friends, at least for now." I did not want to spend any more time with Rawdy's friends anyway, so it was easy to promise him that, but it was going to be much harder to stay away from Rawdy - who was like a brother to me, and in the last six years since I was first allowed to use the phone, we had talked at least once a week. I did not see how I could avoid him more than five, possibly six days, but maybe that would be long enough for things to cool down.

Dan composed himself, and we started walking toward the school. Before we reached the front doors, Dan said, "Remember, Thursday night is the next gathering meeting, and I'd really like to take you. Will you go with me?"

"I would love to go with you."

8

The Gathering

Thursday night, Dan arrived at my house to escort me to Gilpinton Community Gathering. Dad was having dinner with Aunt Marge which left me home alone waiting on the porch swing when Dan arrived. I scampered to his car before he even had a chance to get out. Dad had given me strict instructions that Dan and I were not to be alone in the house, and I was making sure the possibility never arose.

As we headed to the gathering, my hands were sweating and my heart was racing. I was rather nervous about meeting a new group of people. In the back of my mind, I was convinced they would think I had no idea how to talk to God correctly, and I was positive I did not know God as well as they did. But most of all, I was afraid that God would show them who I was on the inside, and they would not like what they saw. After my insightful conversation with Dan, I could recall other instances when I knew what people were thinking, beyond what they were saying. That got me thinking, and I was instantly struck with fear wondering if God tells every FFJ the thoughts and intentions of other people. The more I fixated on the prospects, the more nervous I became. Maybe it is just the bad stuff God reveals. Oh...great! Now *that is* a pleasant thought.

Our conversation in the car was strained, mostly because I was so nervous. The majority of my answers consisted of simple yes and no. One of his questions caused me even more emotions. "Ruthy, have you talked with Rawdy today?"

Thankfully the answer was a resounding "No." Rawdy had not even tried to talk to me.

We pulled into the circle drive of a large, turn-of-the-century house. It was two, maybe three, stories tall with a large front porch. There were four massive pillars sitting on the concrete porch, stretching up to the second story roof. The exterior was painted white and had gold embossed carvings on every corner and window. I could almost envision Scarlet O'Hara walking out the front door. As we entered the house, my breath was taken away by the sheer size of the foyer. The room was open to the second floor with a very grand staircase, twenty-five feet from the front door. Large, wooden, wing-back chairs were arranged in a wide circle, positioned between the stairs and the front door.

Dan and I were the last to arrive, and there were only four empty seats–two seats were right next to each other, while the other two were across the room from each other. Dan motioned for me to take the seat closest to the door, and he took one across the room. We had not discussed sitting next to each other, but it took me by surprise when he left me alone. If all the empty seats had been alone, then it would have made sense, but there were two seats right next to each other, and yet he chose to sit me between two strangers. I almost bolted for the door when a small, cold hand touched my right hand. I was so nervous that I had not realized Dan sat me next to Sarah. It was her ice cold hand reassuringly patting mine–she knew I was nervous about tonight's meeting. Sarah and I had been discussing the gathering for the past two mornings.

"It's nice to see you here, Ruthy," Sarah exclaimed enthusiastically.

"Hey, Sarah, long time no see," I said sarcastically. Sarah had willingly agreed to be my driver for as long as she was needed. We were actually having a great time, and Dad even decided to give Sarah a little gas money. He was obviously very pleased. This arrangement let him off the hook. It allowed him to delay any decision concerning my car.

I quickly glanced around the room studying the faces for recognition. Up to this point, I had tried not to make eye contact with anyone, which was why I had not noticed Sarah sitting right next to me. I was amazed to find that half of the thirty-five people in attendance were at least familiar faces. Two of my teachers were in attendance, the principal, Dan and Sarah's siblings, plus seven classmates.

Ms. Elizabeth Gilpin, the English Literature teacher, was sitting on my left side. I was not in any of her classes that semester, but I would be taking her class called 'Women in Literature' that winter semester. Mike told me, after the three legged race, that she was the great-granddaughter, four times removed, of the founding father of Gilpinton. She had once been engaged to marry, but he had been killed in a car accident the week after he proposed. That was almost sixteen years ago, and now she was thirty-seven years old and had never been married. It was hard to believe that she was single because she was such a natural beauty–the kind you would imagine every guy would be after. She was average height and slender build with long, blond hair and crystal blue eyes. Ms. Gilpin always had a smile on her face, and all the students wanted to be in her class. She demanded a lot of her students, but she was fair.

My thoughts were interrupted by a short, gray-haired man. He introduced himself as Edmund Clark. He instructed everyone to introduce themselves to the group. I was not the only newcomer; a young couple had also recently moved to the area, and they were joining the group for the first time. After we finished the introductions, Mr. Clark asked us to hold each other's hands, and we opened the meeting with thanks and requests to God. He started and others followed his lead, but not everyone said something, and I did not feel compelled to speak, nor was I uncomfortable in my silence. It lasted about twenty minutes, ranging from a general invitation to God and thanksgiving for all He had done for us, to more specific personal needs of individuals. Mr. Clark ended the time by naming each new person and asking God to protect them until we could meet again.

A guy in his early twenties who played the piano, and a teenage girl from my geometry class who was strumming the guitar, led several worship songs. Dan told me there were usually more musicians, including a bass guitar player, a drummer, and a trumpet player, but for some reason they were not going to be at tonight's meeting. I did not know any of the songs, but they were pretty catchy tunes, and it was easy to follow along as they had the words projected up on a screen with the use of a digital projector.

The worship ended after an hour when Mr. Clark took one of the microphones and started speaking to God. This was not like the earlier time; this was a transition taking us from worship to his speech. Mr. Clark began by reading a section of the words from God, and then expounded using a few personal experiences. It was very interesting, and the time flew. Mr. Clark ended by reading from the Old Testament about a man named Elijah. Elijah asked God to hold back the rain for several years, and it did not rain. God provided Elijah with a river to drink from, and the birds brought him food. After a while, the river dried up, and God told Elijah to go find a woman who would give him water and food. He found the woman, but she informed him that she was about to eat the last bit of her food with her son. Elijah asked her to make him some food first, then she and her son could eat the rest. God had told Elijah that if the woman obeyed him the food would not run out. And, that is exactly what happened. Elijah stayed with the woman. After a while, the woman's son became deathly ill, until finally he stopped breathing. The woman became very mad at Elijah and thought he had caused her son's death. He took the boy up to his room and cried out to God. Then Elijah stretched himself across the boy's body three times crying, "O Lord, my God, let this boy's life come back to him!" The boy came back to life.

Before he put the microphone back on the stand, Mr. Clark asked Dan to come up and give witness to the power of God.

Dan seemed a little nervous and said "um" too many times to be sure, but after a couple minutes he seemed to get into a rhythm, and the words flowed with ease. Even his popular fillers (um, you know, and) slowly disappeared. He was so cute. His idiosyncrasies did not bother me–he could have read the dictionary, and I still would have been eager to listen. Thankfully he was not reading the dictionary, and even though I had heard his story once before, there was a new found understanding.

The text that Mr. Clark had read was almost identical to Dan's story with Sarah being closely identified with Elijah. Even though I knew how his story ended, I could not keep tears from welling up.

As I gazed around the room, it appeared that I was not the only one–there was not a single dry eye in the room. As Dan brought his story to a close, applause erupted from the group. The enthusiasm drew us up out of our chairs with whoops and hollers spreading around the room.

When the adrenaline subsided, and the hugs ended, Ms. Gilpin pulled me aside. "Ruth, I was wondering if you would like to help me bake this Saturday. I volunteer at the local food bank two Saturdays a month baking cookies and cakes, and I could use a little help."

"That sounds wonderful! I love to bake."

"So, is that a yes?"

"Yes…that's a yes. What time Saturday?"

"Well, I've noticed you don't have your own car, so I was thinking that I could pick you up around seven o'clock."

"Seven…oh…Okay."

"Is that a problem?"

Once again my face gave me away. "I'm just not really a morning person, but I'll be bright eyed and bushy tailed waiting for you." Not wanting her to think I was uninterested, I opened my eyes wide and put on a big smile; obviously I was over compensating for my previous expression.

Dan interrupted our conversation. "Ruthy, are you ready to go? Hello, Ms. Gilpin." I noticed that Dan was keeping an eye on our conversation, and he must have jumped in to save me from further embarrassment. The question was whose embarrassment was he trying to prevent–his or mine?

"Hello, Dan. You did a stupendous job tonight. I better get going myself. I will see you both tomorrow."

"Bye, Ms. Gilpin. I'm looking forward to Saturday."

Dan looked at me with quizzical eyes and asked, "What's Saturday?"

"Ms. Gilpin has asked me to help her bake for the food bank this Saturday. I thought it sounded like fun...I do like to bake, and it would be nice to know her a little better. Plus, charity work is always an asset on a college application."

"You don't have to convince me, Ruthy. I like Ms. Gilpin, and I think this is a good thing...you could use a role model like her."

"Well, I thought maybe you had arranged this whole thing. Are you telling me it wasn't your idea?"

"No. I had nothing to do with this."

"Oh...really."

"Promise."

He put his arm around my shoulders, and we headed for his car. He opened my door, and I slid in. But before he could get in, Sarah was running toward the car yelling for us to wait.

"Wait. Please wait!"

"What's the problem, Sarah?"

Sarah bent forward and lifted her right hand saying, "Let me catch my breath." After a moment she continued explaining, "Ruthy, I'm not able to pick you up tomorrow morning. Mr. Clark just asked me to do him a favor in the morning. Can you take Ruthy to school tomorrow, Dan? I really am sorry, but I just can't say no to him."

"Don't worry about it, Sarah. I don't mind taking Ruthy to school."

"Yeah...don't worry about it. I don't think either of us minds." I smiled at Dan and gave him a wink.

"Ok...good...I just didn't want to leave you stranded. Have a good night." Sarah ran back to the house, and we drove away.

"Dan, you did a wonderful job tonight. Did you know that Mr. Clark was going to ask you to speak?"

"Yes, of course I did. Mr. Clark spoke with me in the hospital and asked if I would give witness tonight. You really think I did okay?"

"No, you didn't just do okay...you did fantastic. Couldn't you tell by the applause and the screaming? There wasn't a dry eye in the place."

"Well, thank you. I was concerned about getting all the facts straight. I wasn't watching the people's reactions."

"Even though I'd already heard the story, this time was even better with the reference to Elijah and the dead boy. Your story is just like the one in the words from God—as if it's still being written in modern day."

"Ruthy, it is. There is nothing in the Word of God that couldn't still happen today. The old stories act as a guide to strengthen our faith and guide our lives. Nowhere in the Word of God does it say "The End." Dan ended his statement as a matter of fact, all the while pointing his finger at me.

Before I knew it, we had reached my house. The lights were on, and I could see my dad sitting in the living room watching TV. I hated to see Dan leave, but I knew my dad would be counting down the minutes until I got into the house. I was sure that he had been peeking out the window for the past half hour. Dan beat me to the punch line saying, "Ruthy, I hate to call it an evening, but I think someone is waiting on you...plus I'll be seeing you early in the morning."

I opened my door and jumped out exclaiming, "See you in the morning!" Dan waited in the car as I skipped to the front door. When I placed my hand on the door knob, I turned around to gaze at Dan one last time tonight. He was staring at me, grinning, and waving goodbye. I waved back and headed into the house. I heard him drive away as I closed the door.

It was almost ten o'clock as I entered the house and informed Dad that tomorrow my chauffeur would be Dan. He did not seem to mind nor act surprised. He nodded and said, "Sounds like a plan. Goodnight, honey." I was rather surprised by his lack of response or interest in how the meeting went, so I followed his gaze to the TV and understood why I could not turn his attention away from the game—his favorite team, the Kansas City Chiefs, was in its final quarter with a score of twenty to twenty-one. I did not take the time to notice who they were playing, purely from my lack of interest in sports.

I slid into bed at eleven o'clock after completing my nightly routine. It was late enough I should have been able to sink into a deep sleep, but I could not stop my mind—it was full of excitement, anticipation, and a vision of a remarkable young man. I was watching, in my mind, a vivid montage of moments I had spent with Dan when I heard my window crack. The crack was only a small divot with a hairline break approximately an eighth of an inch, but I was perplexed as to what would make it break in such a way. Just then, a small beam of light came shining through my window. It was Sarah, holding a small flashlight. She was motioning for me to come down.

I ran down the stairs, trying not to alert my dad to the late night visitor. I slid out the front door without being detected. Even if my dad had noticed, I was sure he thought I was simply going after my iPod again. Sarah would not come into the house, but insisted on me freezing on my front porch.

"What did you throw at my window? It has a small crack now."

"I'm sorry. I was looking for something to throw at your window–you have a paved driveway. Anyway, I found my brother's BB gun in the car and thought I could throw a BB at your window. I couldn't even get the BB up to your window, so I got the bright idea to use his BB gun. It wasn't such a good idea."

"Oh, don't worry about it. What was so important that you couldn't just call?" I did not want to worry her, but I knew my dad would not be happy about the window. I would have to figure out a way to hide it from him for as long as possible.

"Well, you know when you have something important on your mind how you don't always think rational? I never thought about my cell phone instead of the BB gun until just now, but I had to speak to you in person."

I was not surprised that she had not instinctively thought to use her cell phone because in this small little town there was no cell phone tower. The nearest one was five miles away. Needless to say, you see a lot of people holding their cell phones up in the air trying to get a bar or two.

"It's alright. So what's so important?"

"I spent the last hour talking to your cousin. Ruthy, you have to talk to Rawdy."

"I promised Dan I wouldn't go around Rawdy alone, at least not right now. Besides, I don't think that's such a good idea either."

Sarah became increasingly distraught, begging me to hear her out. Tears started to stream down her cheeks as she began to say, "Ruthy, your cousin needs you. You are the only one that can show him the Way."

"I've never done that before. What would I say? I don't have the words from God memorized like you and Dan."

"You know the Truth and the Way. You don't have to have it memorized to lead someone to Jesus. All you need is God's Spirit and His power."

"Sarah, please! You or Dan should do this. Dan asked me to stay away from him, and I can't go back on my word." I was wondering how long that argument would suffice.

Sarah finally understood my resolve, as a deep sadness and fear swept over her face. She was crying uncontrollably and grabbed my arms begging, "Please, Ruthy...please!"

"Explain this to me, Sarah. I love him as my brother, and I want him to know the Truth as much as anyone, but what is this to you?" I was starting to get frustrated that Sarah would not take "no" for an answer.

Sarah let go of my arms and slowly sat on the porch steps. She was able to compose her voice as she spoke. "I don't know how much you learned in California, or how much Dan has told you, but God gives His Spirit to each one of us who believes in Him, and along with that He gives His anointing power. Most of us share just the basic empowering, but then some of us have special giftings. I am one of those with a special gifting."

"You are? What can you do? Do you know people's intentions or innermost thoughts?" It does not seem like Dan had told Sarah anything about me, and while I was hesitant to share about myself, I was more than a little curious to hear her special gift.

"No. I don't know those things. God shows me what people can be."

"I don't understand. Do you mean you can see the future?"

"Oh no, I don't know or see the future. God allows me to see, in my mind, a picture of what people can become. It's kind of like being able to see who a person will grow up to be."

"Who will I become?"

"It doesn't work that way. God has to show it to me. I don't turn it off and on. I don't choose, and so far it has only been people that are in my circle of influence over a year."

"So you've seen Rawdy *grown up*?"

"Yes, you could say that. Oh, Ruthy, you have to know what an amazing guy he is, and what he could be if he just knew the Way."

"Doesn't he need to know the Truth first?"

"He does. Don't you remember he was there with us when Dan told his story? He knows the Truth of Jesus and has personally seen the Truth in action. All he needs is for you to show him the Way."

"He only knows the Truth in part. Why can't you show him? Obviously you have the passion and desire."

"Ruthy, you can do it. It's easy. He doesn't have to know all the Truth at first. He just needs to know that God loves him so much that He sent His one and only Son to redeem him from sin. If Rawdy surrenders his life to Jesus and turns from his evil ways, then he will live in God's presence forever. Jesus is the Way to salvation–to God. God wants to fellowship with us today, not just when we get to heaven."

"Sarah, I know all that, but Rawdy seems to be on your heart, so I think you should do it."

"I tried." Sarah's face fell into her hands, and she began sobbing again. "He only trusts you, Ruthy."

I put my hand on Sarah's shoulder and said, "What is up between you and Rawdy?"

"It's hard to explain. We're hardly friends, but he knows there's a connection between the two of us that goes beyond the small amount of contact we've had. I was five years old when God showed me who Rawdy would grow up to be, and as a young pre-teen, an immense love grew inside of me for him."

"You love him?"

"You can say it. I know it's completely wrong. He didn't believe the Truth or know the Way, and everyone thinks I'm crazy, but I can't help myself. Yet, the action is there none the less."

"The action?"

"Well, love is not just a feeling. If it's real love then it's backed by actions."

9

The Child

It took another hour to convince Sarah I was not going to talk to Rawdy, at least not before I cleared it with Dan. I did not want to admit to her, but I was more than a little scared of Rawdy's friends, and I did not fully trust him to protect me at the moment. I knew I would have to face Rawdy sometime, but I was not ready that night.

Friday morning, Dan was at my house bright and early. Dad met him at the door and invited him in for breakfast. Most mornings I was doing well to get a bowl of cereal, but Dad got up early and had biscuits and sausage gravy waiting for us. Dan was finished eating his second helping before I had even finished my one and only serving. He must have a furnace for a metabolism. As we were walking out the door, Dad reminded Dan he would be making dinner Monday night. Monday was the night of the big game. I enjoyed any chance I had to spend time with Dan, but my dad's involvement was disconcerting.

School was pretty much the usual humdrum except for the minor detail of Mr. Caldwell using a menthol rub instead of his usual petroleum jelly. Most of the class seemed to be experiencing the common head cold, that is, all except for the members of the FFJ group. I had noticed once before how healthy they all seemed.

I decided to file that information away in my brain for further contemplation and discussion.

After school I spoke with Ms. Gilpin for a few minutes, ironing out the final details for Saturday. We were still standing in the foyer when my dad drove up. Dan's friend had pleaded with him to do a special tutor session after school, so consequently, Dan asked my dad to pick me up rather than expose me to Sarah's pleading again. I expected my dad to wait for me in the truck, but before I knew it, he was standing beside me talking to Ms. Gilpin. Evidently, they had been introduced at the Pumpkin Fest. My dad seemed pleased that I would be spending time with her and insisted she come over early and eat breakfast with us Saturday morning. To my surprise, she agreed.

When we got home, I noticed a large tarp draped over something that resembled a car. I was elated. Did he actually buy me a car? I let out a small giggle in excitement. My dad appeared perplexed until he saw me peek under the tarp. He had never been one to give his emotions away by the looks on his face.

"Oh, honey, it's not what you think."

"And what am I thinking?"

"This is not a *new* car for you."

I was dejected by his words and said, "It isn't?" I was fighting back tears until he finished his explanation.

"Well, it can be your car if we can get it fixed up." He yanked the tarp off the old dusty car. "This was my first car, a nineteen seventy-three, two door, blue, Chevy Nova. The body is still in excellent condition, and it has less than a hundred thousand miles on the engine, but the radiator needs to be replaced, and the heater core is leaking. There are a few other minor issues we can tweak as we go. The master cylinder probably needs to be replaced too. It was a small car in its day, but unlike today's vehicles, it was built with real metal, not plastic. If you must grow up, I'd feel safer with you driving a sturdy car like this."

I stood on my tiptoes, grabbed my dad around the neck, and squeezed as hard as I could, trying to show my immense gratitude. While most girls–for that matter, most people–would not understand what a heater core or a master cylinder was, I did because Dad and I always worked on things together around the farm. Dad always said my hands were smaller and could fit into tight spots easier. I think he just liked being the foreman better than the flunky. This would be the second master cylinder I would be working on and the third heater core. I was not looking forward to the heater core replacement. You can get a nasty headache doing that one. In the end, I suppose I would stand on my head for hours if I ended up with a car.

"Thanks, Dad. This is so amazing! How long will it take us to get it running?"

"I think we can have you safely and legally on the road by the end of the month. We might have to order a few parts and even go to some salvage yards, but I am confident that we can get it done."

"You're the greatest, Dad! I can't wait to show Dan and Sarah."

"What about Rawdy, Little Miss? Your aunt and uncle have been storing this car for me, and when I went to pick it up, Rawdy assured me he would be over to help work on it sometime next week."

"Of course...Rawdy can help too." I was trying not to let my face show my concern. I did not want him to suspect there was anything wrong between Rawdy and myself. Up to that point I had not been able to explain the situation to Dad, and I was not coming up with a good one at that moment either. Trying to change the subject, I asked, "When can we start working on it?"

"Tomorrow, if you like."

"Really?" As soon as the word came out of my mouth, reality set in, and I remembered I had volunteered to help Ms. Gilpin bake for the food bank. "Oh, Dad, I can't work on it tomorrow. I have that thing with Ms. Gilpin."

"That's okay, honey. We can start working on it as soon as you get back if you like. Besides, we'll have to wait on a few parts before we can do any major repairs. Listen, I'll start checking it over tomorrow while you're gone and try to get a parts list put together."

"Thanks, Dad."

"Honey, I've heard really good things about Ms. Gilpin, and I feel this will be good for you."

"She seems like a genuine person, and you know how I love to bake."

Dad put his arm around my shoulder and said, "Come on. Let's go inside. It'll be dark soon, and it's too cold to be standing around out here. Plus, I'm sure you have a few phone calls to make."

He was right. I could hardly wait to call Sarah and Dan with my big news. I would miss my morning talks with Sarah, but I was sure she would rather not have to wait on me everyday. Dan would still insist on me riding with him from time to time, or at least I hoped he would. We were not officially anything more than friends, but if I never rode with him again I would immensely miss our close proximity in his vehicle. Even just sitting next to him made me feel better. As the thoughts percolated in my brain, my stomach began to churn, and I just wanted to lie down. I did not even care if I told Dan about my car, and even the car did not seem as exciting. What good is it to have a car if you cannot enjoy it with anyone? I did not want to chance talking with Sarah again until after I had spoken with Rawdy, but since Dan was helping a friend study for his SAT's, I could not discuss setting up a meeting with Rawdy until tomorrow.

Right then, it hit me: it was just a few weeks ago when I was devastated by the contemplation of my life without Rawdy, and here I was doing that exact thing. A couple of months ago he would have been the first person I would have called, and he would have been right here beside me begging my dad to start work on the car tonight. Yet, there I was alone and too petrified to call him. Life has a funny way of turning upside down before you know it. Up to that point, I had not really missed Rawdy, but in that moment I could not wait to see him or hear his voice. Dan had persuaded me to wait and talk to Rawdy next week, some evening when Dan could join us. I had agreed, mostly out of fear, but also from my strange joy of procrastination. The longer I could postpone the confrontation with Rawdy, the better, or at least that is what I thought earlier that morning. Right then, I wanted nothing more than for the whole thing to be over, and for life to go back to normal.

My dad interrupted my contemplation of the dilemma, calling me downstairs to set the table for dinner. The rest of the night went rather fast. I decided to give my brain a rest and work on a project I started a little over a week ago. I had started crocheting a hat for myself and was hoping to finish it before Saturday. My mom taught me to crochet as a young girl, but I never got beyond the basic chain stitch. Knitting and crocheting had become fashionable the last couple years, so I purchased a book at a local store which promised you could teach yourself. Remarkably, I had been able to follow the directions and read the patterns. That hat was my first project, yet it was turning out nicely and actually looked like the one in the book. Aunt Marge had given me a few pointers along the way, including some encouraging words on my vast array of talents. Little did she know how vast my talents really were!

Saturday morning rolled around way too fast. The only upside to an early weekend morning was my dad's famous, blue-ribbon pancakes. Every time he cooks with one of his recipes, he insists on explaining the secret of the recipe–his pancake recipe was no different. This time he explained how essential it was to whip the egg whites in order to achieve a light and fluffy pancake, and there was something else about almond flavoring being his secret ingredient. I never really cared what his secret was; I just loved to eat them. Once I tried to explain how most families simply open a box of mix and add water, but of course that would never do for my dad. I could already smell the wonderful sweet smell of the pancakes in my bedroom. My stomach growled, and my mouth started to water. It was as if the pancakes were calling me, and my body was answering them back.

By the time I reached the kitchen table, Ms. Elizabeth Gilpin was already there with a half eaten stack of pancakes.

"Good morning, Ruthy!"

"Good morning, sunshine. Are you ready for your pancakes?" Dad was handing me the jug of milk before I even had a chance to sit down.

"Good morning. Yeah, I'm ready." That was the first time I had spoken that morning, and my voice was thick and scratchy.

"Would you like some of this wonderful maple syrup, Ruthy?" Elizabeth grabbed the glass Mason jar, full of syrup, and passed it to me.

"Thank you, Ms. Gilpin."

"I can't believe you made this syrup, Eli. You are such a talented cook."

"Don't even get him started. He has a special recipe for everything, and if you stick around long enough, he will tell you all of them." I was laughing as I explained to Ms. Gilpin, yet I was completely serious.

"I would love to hear some more of those secret recipes sometime, Eli." Ms. Gilpin was staring at my dad with a strange smile on her face.

Little did she know what she was getting herself into, but for some reason I got the distinct feeling she did not care. I knew better and was sure she would come to regret her decision. Dad was generally a very kind person who thought of others before himself, but if you ever got him started talking about one of his recipes, you had better be ready to save yourself. Because if that wild bus, you know, the one that goes around "accidently" killing people on Sunday evenings, passed by your way, and if it was up to my dad to save you, well, you've had it and might as well be named "road kill".

I knew I had to save Ms. Gilpin from herself, so I scarfed down my breakfast and got Dad to help me find my favorite jeans. He was always organized and had everything planned out to a "t", but laundry was his downfall. It was a good thing we had a laundry room with a door to close it off from the rest of the house so we could hide our disgrace. It would take Dad at least five to ten minutes to find my work jeans, which in turn, would give Ms. Gilpin enough time to finish her breakfast.

We reached the food bank right on time. My plan had worked, and Ms. Gilpin explained to Dad that he would have to share his secrets another time. Dad was very pleased; he rarely had such an enthusiastic audience. They even set a date to meet and discuss his secret recipes. Poor Ms. Gilpin. I had tried to save her from that dismal fate, but she had persisted, and I could do no more.

I was overwhelmed by the magnitude of the food bank's mission. The building itself was enormous, with stacks of food ten feet high and six feet deep, and there were at least twelve stacks stretching fifty feet long.

The food bank provided two meals a day, five days a week, and three meals a day, Saturday and Sunday. Ms. Gilpin and I were volunteering to bake the desserts for the afternoon and evening meals for both Saturday and Sunday. I had never seen such large mixers or mixing bowls, and I had no clue you could buy butter in five pound boxes, or sugar in fifty pound sacks. Everything I knew about baking was put to the test with such oversized batches. The food bank had received several large donations from Ms. Gilpin's family which allowed them to build a separate kitchen designated just for baking–it was a baker's dream. There seemed to be an endless supply of baking pans of all shapes and sizes, and they even went as far as to have stone bakeware. There were seven commercial ovens, two range tops, two commercial dishwashers, five sinks, two microwaves, and a very large walk-in refrigerator and freezer.

The order of the day was to start by making angel food cakes, then pumpkin pies, and ending with an assortment of ten different cookies. Ms. Gilpin said we should be done by six o'clock that evening, which would be just in time for the evening meal. My head was spinning with the prospect of making so many desserts in one day. Ms. Gilpin said, "We might have a few helpers off and on during the day, but for the most part it will just be the two of us." She was right about the last part.

We had baked all the pies and half of the cakes before I was able to relax and feel comfortable around Ms. Gilpin. She was a beautiful woman with a gentle, sweet spirit. We were half way through the angel food cakes when she said, "Ruthy, for today you may call me Elizabeth. We are on level playing ground here, and it simply feels wrong for you to call me Ms. Gilpin, and we are not far enough south for you to call me Miss Elizabeth."

"Ok, Elizabeth." I reluctantly spoke her first name, knowing that my dad would not like me being so informal with a teacher. "Ms....I mean Elizabeth, can I ask you a question?"

"Sure, Ruthy. What is it?"

"How old are you?"

"Well, let me see. I'll be...thirty-seven this next year."

"Have you ever been married?"

Ms. Gilpin snorted and flour flew up in her face. Her face was covered in a white chalky dust, and she started to laugh. I could hardly believe she was thirty-six years old; she barely looked twenty-six. She had no visible wrinkles, and she was always dressed in the most recent fashion with the latest hairstyle.

She was still laughing when she said, "No, Ruthy, I've never been married."

"I hope you don't mind me asking. It's just that you are so young looking and so beautiful that I have a hard time believing what everyone says about you."

"And what is everyone saying about me?"

I suddenly got sick to my stomach and wished I had kept my mouth shut. "Oh, nothing really. They told me you were in your mid-thirties, but I didn't believe them. They also told me that you have never been married."

"Well, that is all true."

"Plus there was something about a tragic love story." I really hoped that she would expand on my last point.

"Oh, so they've told you about Clayton Rush."

"Well, I guess. I've never heard his name before, and they didn't seem to know how he died exactly."

"Clayton Rush met his untimely demise at the very young age of nineteen."

"How old were you?"

"Hmmm . . . let me see. I was a senior in high school, and the accident happened in the spring, so I would have been . . . eighteen."

"Were you in love with him?"

"Yes, yes, I do believe I was." She grabbed a tea towel and wiped the flour from her face, motioning for me to join her for a short rest and a glass of sweet ice tea. After a couple large gulps of tea, Elizabeth settled back and began telling me her tragic love story. As I listened, the story unfolded like a movie in my mind.

They met when his family moved to Gilpinton when Elizabeth was fifteen years old. Clayton had his driver's license and was in possession of a brand new, candy apple red, Jeep Wrangler with a black soft top. Clayton had two younger sisters, one of which was Elizabeth's age, Sara, and the other was eleven years younger. The youngest, Emily, was adopted. Elizabeth's parents had encouraged her to befriend Sara. She did not mind because she had developed a crush on Clayton the moment she laid eyes on him. A friendship with Sara would mean time with him, but Clayton was an introverted loner, and it took months before he noticed her, and even then her parents refused to let her date until she was eighteen.

As the years went by, her attention did not waver from Clayton, but his seemed to come and go with the numerous girls he dated. Until one day her father brought up the subject of dating.

Six months before her eighteenth birthday, Elizabeth's parents came to her with a request from a young man. Her father said that after talking with this young man, and realizing his sincere affection and upstanding character, they had decided to allow her to date early. Elizabeth was so excited and convinced herself it must be Clayton. She was surprised her parents would choose the word "upstanding" to describe Clayton's character, she sure would not have. She was not going to be the one to correct them; doing so would risk losing her privilege to go on the date. Her parents had arranged everything–he would come to her house to pick her up on Saturday around six o'clock. They would go to a nice Italian restaurant and to the local community theater where they were performing "Pride and Prejudice", the musical.

When the doorbell rang and her father greeted the young man, it was Elizabeth that was speechless as he entered the room.

The young man was not Clayton Rush, but Marc Whittle–he was her gathering leader's son. Marc was a month older than Elizabeth and had incubated a crush on her since kindergarten. She thought he was a nice looking gentleman with a good temper and a strong character, but she had never desired anything more than a friendship with him. Elizabeth had no choice but to follow through with the date.

Elizabeth was just as surprised as her parents were when she announced they would be going on another date. Elizabeth found herself rather taken by this uninteresting young man. There was nothing overstated about him, and his dreams were nothing out of the ordinary, but his warmth and kindness had struck a chord with her.

Elizabeth and Marc continued to see each other for three months until one night they ran into Clayton at the pizza parlor. Clayton erupted into a fit of fury at the sight of them holding hands. He knew that Elizabeth was not yet eighteen and could not believe that she had gone out with someone else.

Elizabeth took him aside and tried to calm him down. She reminded him that he had been out with many girls in the last few years. He was disgusted to find out she had been seeing Marc for several months. Obviously, Sara had not passed the news on to him. At the shocking news, he turned away from her, and his body began to tremble. She thought he was laughing at her. She pulled him around to face her again only to discover that he was not laughing, but crying. Her heart broke for him, and her desire for him was once again rekindled. It was not long before Marc came looking for her, but not before Clayton asked Elizabeth on a date, to which she agreed.

Elizabeth asked her parents the next day if she could go out with Clayton, and her father said, "Absolutely not. No!" His reasoning was based on the fact that she was not yet eighteen. Precedence had obviously not been set. Her parents also explained their displeasure with Clayton's character, and most of all the fact that he was not a believer, such as they were. She devised a plan to keep her date with Clayton.

After only a few dates, Elizabeth's conscience started kicking in, and she was no longer able to bear deceiving her parents. Elizabeth decided to tell her parents everything–she was only a month from her eighteenth birthday and would be able to date whomever she wanted, or so she thought. They were not at all happy with her decision to dump Marc and pursue Clayton. Her father reminded her that she was not yet eighteen and would have to wait, but he did not stop there. He explained to her, once again, why she must marry a believer. She was a believer and the special Gilpin.

Her parents forbade her from ever going out with him again, but she could not resist the attraction. Elizabeth and Clayton secretly dated for three months. One Saturday in April, he asked her to marry him, and despite her better judgment, she said yes. She knew her parents would never consent to their union. They knew it would be hard without her parents' consent, and with her barely eighteen, but the alternative was unbearable. The next Friday afternoon, Clayton met Elizabeth at the door of her last class. He was obviously upset, but not with her. His mother had asked him to come and pick up his younger sister from school, then take her to dance class. Clayton had planned a romantic evening for Elizabeth–she later found out that he had an engagement ring he was going to give her that night. Elizabeth was later told that he had gotten into an argument with his mother, but grudgingly chauffeured his sister. Halfway to the dance studio, Clayton, still enraged, started arguing with Emily and crossed the center line. His jeep struck a semi truck head on, and they were both killed instantly.

"I was a fool, Ruthy. I wasted a year of my life mourning him. I allowed that emptiness to eat me up when I had the answer all the while. It wasn't until I gave my life back to Jesus that I had peace again. I knew Clayton wasn't a believer, and that fact is what tormented me the worst. I had a chance to tell him about my Lord and Savior, and I had not done it. I was more worried about dating him than his very soul. I've had more trouble living with that fact than with the fact that I've never married. I know other people had told him about Jesus, but he and I were closer than any of those other people, and he might have listened to me. I've made my peace with God, and I've been able to go on, but if I could go back and change it, I would." Ms. Gilpin wiped a tear from her face and stood up, mixing the next cake batter.

She said she had dated other men, but none such as Clayton. None she wanted to marry. Marc went on to become a gathering leader and moved to California with his wife.

By two o'clock, we had completed all the angel food cakes and the pumpkin pies. I lost count after the first twenty of each dessert. Ms. Gilpin warned me that the cookie baking would keep us on our toes, and she was not kidding. Each batch of cookies only took eight minutes to bake, so we were constantly moving pans in and out of the ovens. Remarkably, we finished baking the cookies an hour ahead of schedule. Ms. Gilpin said that was a new record, and she would love for me to come back next weekend. I graciously tried to bow out, but I am not sure I was totally successful.

When we were finally able to sit down and relax, I asked her another question.

"Why were you not allowed to date Clayton? What did they mean by you being a 'special Gilpin'?"

"Well, I'm actually not the 'special one'...that would be my child."

10

Space-Time Continuum

I was just about to ask Ms. Gilpin the details of her child when a crowd of workers flooded the room. A large gentleman entered the room wearing a chef's hat and an apron exclaiming, "Ladies, you've done a phenomenal job! I can't imagine how you baked all those desserts in such a short amount of time."

"Thank you, Mr. Arnold, for your high praises. I couldn't have done it without Ruthy, and I really should thank her for her help, but we're only about an hour ahead of schedule," explained Ms. Gilpin.

"My dear, I know you and Ms. Beverly Mae are usually very fast, but I don't think you've ever gotten all the baking done before one o'clock."

"One o'clock?"

"Yes, dear. It's one o'clock. We've just finished serving the last lunch meal."

"But that clock says five-thirty," I pointed out to the crowd.

"Yes, Ruthy, it does, but that clock hasn't been keeping good time for years. Haven't you ever noticed, Elizabeth?"

Ms. Gilpin was silent for a few moments and then said, "I guess we have always used the timers on the individual ovens, and Ms. Beverly Mae always wears a watch."

I was not a mathematician, but I could add well enough to know there was no possible way we could have baked over forty pies and cakes in only seven ovens, plus over forty dozen cookies, in only five and a half hours. Then there was the fact that we had taken a rather long break when she told me the story of Clayton Rush.

Mr. Arnold was the first to speak, "I think we've all just witnessed a miracle."

The crowd erupted into a joyous celebration. People were jumping around, dancing, clapping, and there were deafening screams piercing my ears. When the crowd finally calmed a little, I sheepishly asked, "What kind of miracle do you mean?"

Mr. Arnold sat me down and explained that there was no possible way for science to explain what had just happened. We could not possibly have baked all those goods in just over five and a half hours. God must have prospered our time. "Ruthy, I'm not sure how God did it, but I know this was a genuine miracle!" exclaimed Mr. Arnold.

Mr. Arnold looked at Ms. Gilpin and exclaimed, "Elizabeth, if these signs and wonders keep following you, I do believe you'll fulfill that prophesy!"

"Mr. Allen, I've never had any such thing happen to me before. Something tells me that Ruthy was more than a little responsible for God showing us mercy." Ms. Gilpin walked over to me and put her hand on my shoulder saying, "Ruthy, have you ever experienced such a thing before? Do you know why this might have happened today?"

I had never felt more ignorant than at that very moment. I had no idea what just happened, or how I could have been involved with its phenomenon. "I really don't know how to answer that,

Elizabeth. I've never had time stand still or speed up, or whatever this may have been, for me before."

"But your father has told me that you have experienced some supernatural occurrences. Right?"

"Yes...I guess you could call them that."

Mr. Arnold was excited by that revelation and tried to pry more information out of me, but Ms. Gilpin interrupted him.

"Ruthy, did you ask God for help so that we could get done early today?" Ms. Gilpin was kindly asking the questions, and yet it seemed like an accusation more than a question.

"Well...yes, I did, but it wasn't that I didn't like baking with you. I had a great time and really enjoyed hearing your story. I enjoy baking, but the thought of almost twelve hours of baking in one day seemed overwhelming. So, I said a little request to God asking Him to make this go fast. I thought He might send us a few more workers so we could get done quicker, but as you know, we only had two people help us, and they were only here for about a half hour. I came to the conclusion that God heard me but didn't think it was that important in the scheme of all the world's issues." The room was in an uproar, everyone was laughing hysterically.

Mr. Arnold took the opportunity to explain things to me. "Well, my dear, I do believe God answered you. He just didn't do it the way you thought He should. I can't explain it all, but there is nothing too big or too small for the Lord. Your faith has made this happen, Ruthy. Elizabeth, where did you ever find this amazing young woman?"

"She is Eli's daughter."

"Oh...well, that is very interesting isn't it. Ruth, you might turn out to be more like your namesake in the Bible than you ever thought." Mr. Arnold grabbed a hold of my shoulders and was squeezing as he spoke my given name.

I was more than shocked to hear Mr. Arnold call the words from God, the Bible. I decided it must have something to do with his age. I was also very surprised that Ms. Gilpin referred to my dad by his first name, as if Mr. Arnold knew him personally. To my knowledge, my dad had never been to the food bank before, nor had he ever spoken of Mr. Arnold. These issues, plus a few comments from Ms. Gilpin, had my mind rushing with questions, searching for some kind of normalcy. Next thing I knew, I was lying on the floor with the crowd of people looking down at me. Of course, I fainted. Ms. Gilpin had a cool wash cloth on my forehead, and Mr. Arnold was leading them in a request to God for me.

As I was ascending from the black tunnel, the first thing I heard was Ms. Gilpin saying, "Eli says this is common for her."

I tried to lift my head, but someone's arms were holding me down. "Ruthy, stay put for a little longer. Your head hit the tile floor pretty hard. Can you talk yet?"

I recognized the voice to be Ms. Gilpin, and I tried to respond. "I'm sorry. This seems to happen to me way too often. I'm okay. I'd like to sit up now, please." One of the volunteers was a doctor, and he kindly checked me over from head to toe, giving me a clean bill of health.

After doting on me another ten or fifteen minutes, Mr. Arnold urged Ms. Gilpin to take me home. I was feeling much better, but I was ready to be back home and away from all the staring. Ms. Gilpin insisted on walking me to my house. Dad met us at the door but was not surprised when Ms. Gilpin explained that I had fainted. I insisted I was fine and did not need help up to my room.

My brain was still spinning with the events of the day, and I was hoping for some time alone to process it all.

As I was walking up the stairs Ms. Gilpin exclaimed, "I hope you're willing to help me again in two weeks?"

That was the last thing I was concerned with at the moment and answered almost without thinking, "Sure."

My dad came upstairs around six-thirty with a tray of food. "I wasn't sure if you would be up to eating with us downstairs, so I thought I would bring the food to you."

"Us? Who's down there with you?"

"Ms. Gilpin is still here. It was nearly dinner time when you got home, so I invited her to stay and eat. Is that a problem?" He seemed awfully defensive at my question, but I did not really care who he invited to dinner. It did not matter to me, that was the least of my concerns–Dad was always inviting people to dinner.

"No...I really don't care who you eat with. I just thought she had already gone."

"Watch the attitude, Little Missy. I know you've had a hard day, but that doesn't give you an excuse to be rude."

"Sorry, Daddy. I didn't realize how that came out. Thanks for the food."

"Honey, I thought you might be interested to know that I was able to get the parts list completed today."

"You did?! Really? Wow...thanks, Dad! I can't wait to get started."

"I know. I think it would be best if you rested and tomorrow, maybe after noon, we can start taking off parts."

"Was it as bad as you thought?"

"Well...it wasn't any worse than I'd thought, if that makes any sense."

"So you're saying we can do it ourselves, but it will still probably be the end of the month before I'll be able to drive it."

Dad chuckled a little and answered, "Yes, that is exactly what I'm trying to say. You definitely are a chip off the old block, sweetheart. The master cylinder is shot, and the heater core is leaking."

"Hey, Dad?"

"Yes, dear?"

"Thanks."

Dad did not have to explain to me what a shot master cylinder was, or what a leaky heater core meant to my car. I had spent years on our farm tinkering around with my dad. I knew exactly what it was going to take to replace these items in my Nova. The master cylinder is simply the reservoir for the brake fluid; basically, without it you do not have brakes. That repair would take us a good afternoon–it would not be too bad as long as the brake lines come out easily. It will take longer if we have to replace the brake lines. A leaky heater core reveals itself with a thin layer of antifreeze on your windshield, and usually you will end up with a puddle of fluid on the passenger side rug too. Now this repair, on the other hand, is a significantly more substantial one and will require me to be on my head for several hours. I remember the last time I had to put in a heater core. I had a headache for the rest of the day. To do the job properly, you really need to be a contortionist.

Dad left the room, closing the door behind him. I could not hear any of their conversation, but I was able to hear her car pull away just over an hour later. I stayed up in my bedroom for the rest of the evening. Dad was acting strange. Something was going on with him, and I did not want to endure any more conflict. I easily forgot the events of the evening as my mind drifted back to the "miracle" of the day. Judging by everyone's reaction at the food bank, this kind of thing was not a common occurrence for everyone. Obviously, fainting was not that common either. I had never experienced any tear in the space-time continuum before today, but I had definitely experienced God answering my request. One thing I had learned is that you cannot underestimate the Lord and what He can or will do.

It was after ten o'clock Sunday morning before I awoke. My dad was already gone to his "special time" with Aunt Marge. I was surprised to see Ms. Gilpin's car sitting in our driveway. After searching the entire house, I confirmed that I was alone. I knew something had to be going on, but I had no clue what it was. Well...I am not dumb. I could see that Dad was attracted to Ms. Gilpin, any single man in his right mind would be, but I could hardly believe that Ms. Gilpin would be interested in my dad. He was not a bad looking guy; some women have even called him a stud, whatever that means, but he was several years older than Elizabeth. He had lots of wrinkles and was divorced with a teenage kid, not to mention the fact that he was not a believer. How could she tell me the story of Clayton, and then the next minute consider another non-believer. None of it made sense to me. I am sure she gets lonely at times, plus she told me that she still believed she would get married one day and have children, but . . . my dad!

My contemplation was interrupted by the phone ringing. It was Dan. He had been up tutoring until three o'clock Sunday morning and had just awoken.

"How are you, Sunshine?"

"I'm terrific. You'll never guess what my dad did for me!"

His voice was still thick and hoarse, causing him to clear it halfway through his sentence. "No, I can't imagine what...your dad has done."

"Well, when we got home Friday evening, there was a large tarp in the driveway."

"Your dad gave you a tarp?"

"No, silly. It's what was under the tarp that is exciting."

"Okay...really, Ruthy, I am way too tired for this kind of conversation. Can you just tell me already?"

"Fine!" I was not really upset with him, but a little disappointed in his lack of consciousness.

"My dad gave me a car!"

"Wow! You have a new car?"

"No, not a new car, but it's new to me."

He seemed to be waking up and started chuckling when he said, "Hey, a car is a car. What kind is it anyway?"

"It is a nineteen seventy-three, two door, wedgewood blue, Chevy Nova SS."

"Wow! I am impressed."

"Wait, I'm not done yet. It has a 350 cubic inch V8 engine, and it was one of the last cars to have the two-speed Powerglide automatic transmission."

He was laughing when he responded, "Okay...you've lost me there."

I giggled back, not wanting to out do his knowledge of cars. "Basically that just means it has a high-performance engine, and that was the last year for the Powerglide automatic transmissions." I usually do not like to talk much about mechanics with guys my own age. From previous experience, I found that guys become very defensive, as if they were supposed to be born with some kind of sixth sense about cars and motors. I decided to try and move the conversation along. "Would you like to come over and work on it with us sometime?"

He hesitated a bit, then answered, "I'm really not much of a mechanic."

I regretted making the offer, but I could not find a way to back out, and I did not want to make him feel inferior. "Don't worry about it. If you want to, the offer still stands. Besides, my dad is a great teacher. I hope I haven't said anything wrong. I know some guys get upset when they find out I know more about cars than they do."

"Oh, Ruthy, you don't have to worry about me. I think it's great. I don't mind if you showed me up. I just have two left hands when it comes to working on cars. I would hate to break something."

Dan has always known how to set me at ease. "Thanks! No pressure, but will you at least ride with me when it's all fixed."

"Absolutely. I would love to take it for a spin if I could. Just because I don't know how to fix a car doesn't mean I don't want to drive one."

"So, was there a reason that you called?" I always loved to hear from Dan, but he usually didn't call on weekends, especially Sunday mornings.

"Yes, there is. I talked with Sarah yesterday, and I think it's time we had our talk with Rawdy, and the sooner the better. What are your plans for this afternoon?"

"We're going to start taking parts off of the car as soon as Dad gets back."

"Do you think you could squeeze some time in to talk with Rawdy?"

"As much as I hate confrontation, I think it would be best to get this over with. I'll have to talk with my dad first, but I'm sure if it involves me spending time with Rawdy he'll say that it's fine with him. What time will work for you?"

Dan and I decided to wait for my dad to come home and see what time worked best for him, and then we would go looking for Rawdy. We agreed it might be best if Rawdy did not know we were both coming for this conversation. The less time Rawdy had to stew about what he would say the better it would be.

11

The Figure

The front door opened, and my dad walked in. I had not heard his car drive up, nor did I hear Ms. Gilpin drive away. I could not let the fact that my dad had spent the morning with Ms. Gilpin pass without mentioning something to him.

"So…you and Ms. Gilpin were together all morning?"

I must have caught him off guard.

"Oh, honey! You really got my ticker going. I didn't see you standing there." He turned on his home theater system without saying another word.

"You still haven't answered my question. Or did you think I wouldn't notice?"

"I guess I didn't think it was that big of a deal."

"Dad, really?"

Before I could say anymore the doorbell rang. It was Dan.

"Hello, Ruthy. Hello, sir."

"Hi, Dan. Did you come to help Ruthy work on her car?"

"I wish, sir, but I don't think it would do her much good if I did. I am noted as one of those who, after everything has been put back together, always has a spare part or two."

Dad chuckled a little responding, "I see. You're one of those. Well, invite the boy in, Ruthy, or shut the door, unless you're planning on us heating the neighborhood."

"Please come in, Dan." I lowered my voice and whispered, "I thought I was going to call before you came over."

Dan matched my volume answering, "Plans have changed."

With normal volume, Dan addressed my dad. "Sir, would it be alright if I took Ruthy over to Sarah's house? Rawdy is going to be there along with Sarah's parents."

"Rawdy will be there? Sure, as long as her parents will be there, that'll be fine."

Before I had a chance to say anything, Dan grabbed my coat from the closet, slipping my arms in, one after another, pulling me toward the door. We were on the sidewalk before I was able to say anything. "What is going on?"

"Sarah called me a couple minutes ago and said that Rawdy had called her and was on his way to her house. He wants to talk to you. She said he sounded pretty messed up. Sarah told me that either I could pick you up, or she and Rawdy were on their way over to your house. I promised her we would be there as soon as possible.

"Dan, I feel sick." I wanted to get this conversation over with as soon as possible, but the thought of confronting Rawdy had my stomach churning. I bent forward and put my hands on my knees.

"I've been warned about you, Ruthy. Are you about to faint?"

I straightened myself back to an upright position. "No...what do you mean? Who warned you?"

He could easily see that I was not clammy and had my wits about me, so his alarm started to ease as he responded, "Your dad, Sarah, Ms. Gilpin, and even you have all given me a heads-up that your body has a tendency to express your emotions."

I laughed and touched his forearm. He did not move or ask me to move my hand, but I knew if I left it there any longer things would get awkward. As I lifted my hand, he quickly looked into my eyes and gave me a short grin, then turned his attention back to the road. Dan was a very diligent driver, always aware of his surroundings and cautious with his allowed distractions. He loved his iPod as much as I did, but he never allowed music while he was driving through town.

We were at Sarah's house before I knew it. My stomach started doing summersaults again. Dan grabbed my arm and said, "Everything will be fine. All you have to do is lean on the Lord for help. Heavenly Father, guide our thoughts and our words as we speak with Rawdy. Open his heart to receive what we say, and let his ears plainly hear our words without any confusion from the heavenlies. We declare that Rawdy is a part of Ruthy's family, and no demonic force can stop him from becoming a believer. In Your Son's name, Jesus, we ask and declare these things."

I had always envied Dan's ability to talk with God like he was talking with me, not even aware of the people around him.

"Thank you for those words, Dan."

The front door opened as Dan was reaching for the doorbell. It was Sarah, and she was exclaiming, "What took you so long? Well, come in already. Rawdy's waiting in the game room."

Sarah lived in one of the newer subdivisions of Gilpinton. Her house was described as a McMansion, referring to its shear size and outrageous décor. I had always imagined her hallways went on for miles, but not today–they seemed rather tiny at the moment. Each step brought us that much closer to Rawdy and my day of reckoning. Would I be able to express my relationship with God to someone else? Could I convince Rawdy to believe in Jesus? Could I show him how real He can be in our lives? I was about to find out. Ready or not, here I go.

We stepped through the door of Sarah's game room only to find Rawdy sitting on the brown leather couch, slumped forward, holding his head in his hands. Sarah broke through the silence saying, "Rawdy, Ruthy is here."

Rawdy turned his head toward the door, and I could see his tear stained face. His eyes were bloodshot and swollen with only small slits for openings. Once again I could tell he had not slept much, and he was wearing the same clothes I had seen on him Friday at school. Sarah leaned toward me and whispered, "Prepare yourself. I don't think he has bathed in a few days. You're going to have to get past that fact and die to yourself, Ruthy. I don't want you vomiting on my father's favorite couch."

I was appalled that she would think of me as such a shallow person. I started to respond but decided to let it go. I wondered what opinion these people were getting of me. I guess I would have to give them leeway considering the fact that I had fainted several times since I moved to Gilpinton.

Rawdy snapped me out of my funk saying, "Ruthy, please help me!"

My heart sank with his words. He was desperate.

"I'm here now, Rawdy." Without even thinking, I ran to his side and wrapped my arms around him. He grabbed around my back, burrowing his head into my lap.

"You have to make it stop, Ruthy, please make it stop!"

"Make what stop? What's wrong? Talk to me, Rawdy."

But he made no sound. Instead it was Sarah who answered for him. "He can't sleep, he can't eat, he keeps seeing the night that Dan was beaten, and then there is Mike and Chad."

"What about Mike and Chad?" I hated to hear that Rawdy was still hanging around those guys, but I knew they would not let him alone.

Just then Rawdy lifted his head and sat straight up. "Chad wants to go after Dan again and...and you."

"Me? Why me?"

"Because you're what links Dan and me. At first I was willing to consider knocking off Dan...again." He turned and looked at Dan and said, "Sorry man! I know it sounds crazy." Then he turned back to me and continued explaining. "It wouldn't be an easy thing to see Dan die again, but if it would stop these tormenting nightmares and end our fear of him telling the authorities, then I was willing to consider it. But when they told me that you would have to go too...well...I just couldn't handle it. Ruthy, I think I'm losing my mind."

Dan interrupted and said, "I can see where you're coming from, and I forgive you."

Rawdy responded with a thank you, but he was interrupted by Sarah explaining, "Rawdy hasn't slept for almost a week because he has been sitting outside your house every night, watching out for you. Every day he's with Chad and Mike trying to make sure they don't come after you, Ruthy."

My jaw dropped, and I turned to Rawdy. I was speechless, but even before I could think of a response, Rawdy spoke saying, "I can't go on. I fell asleep last night, and I'm sure Chad and Mike are on to my scheme. I've been trying to call them all morning long, but there is no answer from either one of them. I just spent the last hour searching town. I'm scared that I can't keep you safe any longer. Sarah told me that you were riding with her to and from school, so I would use that time to catch a few z's, but it's catching up with me." He started crying again and put his head back in my lap.

I hated to see a big burly guy cry like such a little baby, but I realized that if I was ever going to have a chance to help him believe in Jesus, this was the time. Carpe Diem, as my English teacher would say, "Seize the day," or as the words of God would say, "For such a time as this."

I tried to think of the right words to say, wishing that I was an eloquent speaker about to say the perfect thing–eloquent is not a term used to describe me. I was more like the babbling idiot who was always stumbling over her words. Just then I remembered what Dan had said right before we entered Sarah's house. I put my head down on Rawdy's and started to speak to God. I realized that I could not fix this. This was much bigger than me, but I did know the answer. My emotions started to overtake me, and tears started to roll down my face onto his hair. My words were shaky at first, but then strength seemed to rise from deep within me. I spoke from my heart, not some rehearsed script. After a few minutes, I could feel his body begin to tremble, and I felt it too. It was like a vibration deep within me.

Soon the room was filled with a white cloud, and a large figure was standing in front of us. The figure walked over to Rawdy and took hold of his hands. The figure appeared to be a male human, yet I knew he was not. Sarah's game room had a vaulted ceiling, and without a measuring stick to judge his height, I guessed him to be close to ten feet tall. For a considerable amount of time he did not make a sound, not even when he walked toward us. I was amazed at how still he was, kneeling there holding Rawdy's hands, and yet, when he moved, I could barely see the transition between positions. It was similar to holding two drawings and flipping forward and backward between them. I could see him standing, and the next nanosecond he was kneeling.

My mind was spinning, trying to understand what my eyes were seeing, and I felt myself starting to go into the dark hole, but I successfully resisted. I realized that the figure had put one of his hands on my arm, and he said, "Ruth." There was no way I was going to lose it now. He had my full and undivided attention. He let go of my arm and grabbed Rawdy. When I looked down at Rawdy, he was staring right at the figure with his mouth wide open. He must not have seen the figure until it said my name. I could feel his body tense even though he was still trembling.

The figure helped Rawdy sit up. Then he spoke, "Do not fear, for I have come to bring you good news. Rawden, God has heard your cries, and He has sent me to answer you. God has a miraculous plan for Ruth's life, and He will protect her so she can fulfill that destiny. He will answer your cries, and your sins are forgiven. You have accepted Jesus as your Savior; now, trust in Him and follow His Way."

He turned to me, yet kept a hold of Rawdy and said, "You are blessed, and God is calling upon you to do a work for Him. Trust in the Lord and in His power. You are more sensitive than others because there is a special purpose for your life. Your father has asked, and God has heard his cry. Learn to control your human emotions while learning to express the Lord's. It's no accident that your emotions are easily expressed through your body. At the right time, God will show you the steps you will take to carry out His plan. Tune your ear to the Lord's voice. Do not fear, but be full of strength."

Just as he had appeared, he was suddenly gone. I looked over at Rawdy, and he was staring straight at me with his eyes wide and his mouth hanging open. I realized that the figure had not spoken to Sarah or Dan. Had they left the room? I glanced over to the spot where I had last seen them, but they were not there. I looked back at Rawdy and asked him, "Where are Dan and Sarah?" He leaned over me to peer over the side of the couch, but never said a thing. Sure enough, they were both lying face down on the floor, not moving a hair. I had not thought about looking on the floor. I wondered what had possessed Rawdy to do so. While we were staring at them, both Dan and Sarah started to pick themselves up. We were all still awestruck by the weight of God's presence and not able to utter a peep. Dan drug his body to the edge of the couch, sitting next to me, while Sarah sat back down on the floor.

"Can you believe what he said?" I asked.

Dan answered me first, leaning close to my ear saying, "I'm sorry. I missed it. What did Rawdy say?"

"I'm not talking about Rawdy. Rawdy didn't say anything."

"I'm confused. If it wasn't Rawdy speaking, then who is the 'he' you are referring to?"

"Don't play games with me, Dan. You know very well who I am talking about."

"No, I'm afraid I don't know who you are talking about."

I looked at Dan and then to Sarah, questioning, "You didn't hear him? Did you see him?"

In unison, they both said, "See who?"

I looked at Rawdy and pleaded with my eyes asking, "Did you see and hear him?"

Thankfully, he excitedly replied, "Oh, of course I did! I heard what he told me, and what he said to you."

Dan and Sarah looked at each other with confusion written on their faces, and then Dan said, "We honestly have no clue what you are talking about. Would you please explain?"

"First things first. What happened to the two of you?" I was not at all convinced I knew what had happened.

Sarah replied this time saying, "I saw a cloud in the room, and the next thing I know, I am getting off the floor without an inkling of how I got there."

Dan agreed with Sarah and pleaded for details.

I was shocked when Rawdy started speaking before I could utter a word.

"Ruthy was saying something to God when this huge dude just appeared in front of us. He had to be nine or ten feet tall. His voice was so strong, but at the same time soft, and he touched my hands. His touch was as soft as a baby, but he was ripped. He spoke to me and told me not to be scared. He said that he would take care of Ruthy, and that she had some kind of destiny to complete."

Rawdy paused and looked at me with a puzzled expression.

I explained, "He didn't say that he would take care of me, Rawdy. He said that God would protect me. That was not God. I'm not sure who the figure was, but I am positive it wasn't God. He also told Rawdy that God had heard his cry and had forgiven him. He continued by saying Rawdy had accepted Jesus as his Savior, and now he was to trust in Him and follow His Way."

Sarah began to cry profusely. I realized what this meant to Sarah. Sarah had always known that Rawdy would one day be a believer, and as such, she could pursue a relationship with him beyond friendship. She laid back down on the floor, curled up into a ball, and I could not imagine an end to her crying anytime soon.

12

A Marriage Proposal

We finally decided it was time to head home after almost two hours of sitting in awe of God. Rawdy carried Sarah to her room–she was still crying. Rawdy rode home with Dan and me, so I was able to ask him what he thought the figure meant when it said that God had heard my dad's cry. Rawdy said, "I remember that being said, but I don't have a clue what it means." Dan stayed noticeably quiet, not giving any kind of opinion on the matter. I wondered if my dad had been crying about me, and God had heard that cry. I resigned to the fact that I probably would not know the answer anytime soon.

"Hey, Rawdy, when did you become a believer?" I asked.

"Well, you know that I've been keeping an eye on you recently."

"Yeah."

"I was in your bushes the night Sarah came by asking you to talk with me. I listened to what you both had to say. It made sense, and with what Dan had said the night of the Pumpkin Fest, I decided to ask for God's forgiveness and for Jesus to be my savior and my redeemer. I wasn't sure if it really took until the figure told me that. I was afraid I might not have said it right or forgotten something."

I tried to keep myself from giggling when I said, "God sees your heart. It isn't a formula. Well, I just want to say that I'm glad."

Rawdy and I were both shocked to see Aunt Marge's car in my driveway when we arrived.

"What is your mom doing at my house, Rawdy?"

"I have no idea. Usually Mom and Dad have their card game Sunday afternoons."

Dan spoke up at that point. "I called your dad, and he then called Rawdy's mother."

"You did what?!" We both exclaimed.

"It was time the four of you talked about this."

"And just what do you think we are going to say to them? How do you explain to a non-believer that there was a ten foot tall figure standing in a game room telling you God sent him?"

Dan got a sly smirk on his face and said, "Well, I don't know what you would say to a non-believer, but to your parents, I would just tell them everything."

Rawdy had exited the car and was starting to open my door when I noticed Dan was not moving, nor had he cut the engine of his car.

"You're not going in with us?"

"Don't worry. You will know what to say. Besides, these are your parents, and I think you all have lots to explain to each other. Ruthy, hear them out and remember to share your heart."

"Please, don't do this to me!" Now more than ever before, I was hoping that my body was giving away my emotions. Words failed me, and I could not explain to Dan how important it was that he be by my side, but I was unsuccessful in my pleading.

Dan leaned across the car and gave me a hug, reassuring me one last time. "You will do fine."

"Get out here, Ruthy. I'm freezing."

Rawdy and I walked to the front door; neither of us knew exactly what to expect. The second we opened the door, my Aunt Marge threw her arms around Rawdy and started crying saying, "Finally, oh my baby! It's finally happened."

Surprisingly, I did not miss out on the parental explosion because my dad also grabbed hold of me, crying and saying something inaudible. I looked over at Rawdy, and we both had the same dumbfounded expression on our face. Things were getting awkward, so I decided to break the silence. "Dad, we have something we need to tell you."

"Oh, honey, we know all about it, and we are so excited."

"Excited about what? How could you know?"

My dad turned to Aunt Marge and nodded his head toward the living room. "I think we should all go sit down and talk."

I knew something was seriously going on when my dad sat down on the loveseat, motioning me to join him. I had never seen my dad sit anywhere other than in his recliner, except when Elizabeth was there. Aunt Marge and Rawdy sat on the couch across the room from us. Dad started by saying, "Honey, after Dan called, we got a call from Sarah's parents explaining the amazing events of this afternoon. Ruthy . . . Rawdy . . . Marge and I are both believers."

Rawdy spoke before he really thought through what he was saying. "What do you two believe?"

"Rawdy, they believe in Jesus like we do!" I could not wrap my brain around the recent revelation. On the one hand, I was excited that my dad was a believer, but on the other hand, I was very confused.

Rawdy, being such a new believer, was naturally overjoyed to find out his mother and uncle were also believers. And let us face it, he had just experienced the most amazing event, possibly of his entire life. "Mom, that is so amazing! Uncle Eli, how long have you been one of us?"

"For almost two years." My dad was answering Rawdy but looking straight at me.

Tears welled up in my eyes and I whimpered, "Two years?"

"I'm so sorry, honey."

I pulled away from him and stood up. "Two years! So you were a believer when everything happened in California? Why didn't you tell me? You let me go through all that feeling that I was alone. Why? I just need to know why?"

Dad reached out to touch me, but I took a step back.

"Honey, I'm so sorry. Please, let me explain. Sit down, and I will tell you everything."

Reluctantly, I sat down, but this time I sat in Dad's recliner. I was trying not to have an attitude or be disrespectful, but at that moment in time I felt completely betrayed. My dad had been the one constant through everything, and now I was finding out that he had not been telling me everything for two whole years. That last year I had felt like such a freak, an outsider, and all alone. Yet, all the while, he knew what I was going through, but he did not give me a lifeline to grab.

"Okay, I'm listening."

"Do you remember the last trip we took here to Gilpinton as a family?"

"Yes, it was in July."

"Your mother and I had been having troubles in our marriage, and I went for a walk with your Aunt Marge. We headed for the park and spent several hours talking about this and that. I really didn't feel that we were accomplishing anything, and I knew your mother would be upset if we stayed out any longer, so we headed back to Marge's house. We were on the north shore when I heard a loud screeching noise coming around the corner. It was a grain truck, and its brakes had failed. The truck ran right over me, and that was the last thing I could remember until I woke up in the hospital."

Aunt Marge interrupted, exclaiming that she could tell the story better since she was not the one that had died. "I heard the noise and saw the truck, but there was no way I could save Eli. As you could imagine, I was devastated and scared out of my wits. The driver of the truck was able to use the emergency brake and bring his truck to a stop. He ran back to us, and then radioed for help, but before the ambulance could get there, the driver started to speak to God as he leaned over your father. I had no idea what he was doing; it was the most bizarre thing I had ever seen. I had already felt for a pulse and looked to see if he was breathing, but Eli was gone. After about five minutes of speaking to God, your father began to breathe again, and his color started to come back. It was then that the man introduced himself to me. He was William Carl Gilpin the sixth. You know his daughter Elizabeth."

My mind was starting to swirl again. Ms. Gilpin's father had saved the life of my dad. My dad had died!

Aunt Marge continued explaining, "The ambulance took ten minutes to get to us, and before it left the accident site, Eli was sitting up talking with us."

My dad interrupted Aunt Marge saying, "Thanks, Marge, I can take it from here. We called your mother from the hospital, and she and your uncle came right over. We didn't want to scare you or

Rawdy, so that's why you never heard anything. By the time your mother got to me, we had gotten back the x-rays, and they could see that almost every bone in my body had been broken, but all the breaks were already healed.

"Mr. Gilpin stayed by my side for hours, and after your mother arrived, he invited us to come over to his house so we could discuss what had occurred. Your mother was reluctant, but I insisted. I knew I had died, and I knew I had been healed, so there was no way I could just bury my head in the sand. Your aunt and uncle came with us to the meeting. The Gilpins invited a few of their friends to meet with us. They took turns explaining to us about God and Jesus, plus they explained that God had healed me and brought me back to life. I was so excited that I asked them what I had to do to become one of them. Marge was just as excited as I was, and they led us in a few words to God and set up training classes for us. Your uncle was a little hesitant, but not resistant. He just needed more time to let it all sink into his brain. Your mother, on the other hand, refused to listen to them anymore, and she walked back to the house. I tried for several days to get her to go to the meetings with me, but she wouldn't.

"When we got back home to Nebraska, I found a group of believers. They were close to a hundred miles away, making it impossible for me to meet with them on a weekly basis. I started asking for books and cd's that could teach me in the Way of Jesus, but each step I took closer to the Lord, your mother took a step farther away from me. She was making me choose, and I had no choice but to go after the Lord. Our marriage really started to unravel when I told her that I was going to start teaching you about Jesus. She threatened to leave me and run away with you. I decided to just drop the issue until I could figure something out.

Eventually, your mother couldn't stand to be around me anymore and left. She tried to take you with her, but I told her that I would fight her for you. I am sorry to say that she told me that she would let me keep you if I would sell the farm and split the money with her. I would've given her the entire farm if I had to, if it meant I could keep you."

Tears filled his eyes, and he cleared his throat then continued with the story. "Without the farm, I had to find a way to support us, so a fellow believer offered me a job in California. I was a mess after your mother left, and I could hear you crying yourself to sleep every night. Honey, I felt like such a failure, and all I knew to do was ask God for help. I'm sorry, but I let fear get the best of me, and I thought that if I told you about Jesus that you would leave me like your mother did. I know I was wrong to do that, but I just couldn't handle you leaving me too."

My dad's words stung like ice. I had been so wrong about my dad. How could I be mad at him? I had the same fear that my dad would leave me if I had told him about being a believer. I had no right to judge him when I had done the same thing. I got up out of the chair and sat back down next to him. He grabbed my hand and kissed my check.

"Dad, please continue."

"I found a fellowship group in California and realized one of the teachers at your school was also a member. I knew you were having a hard time without your mom and with the transition, so I asked her to invite you to the youth events. She was more than willing to watch over you. She tried to encourage me to tell you about myself, but even though I knew you were starting to believe, the fear still had a grip on me, and I just couldn't talk to you. I was happy that you were growing in your faith, and for the moment that was enough for me. When we moved here I should have told you, but once again, I let the fear stop me."

He stopped talking and took hold of my face. "Please forgive me. I started going to meetings with your Aunt Marge the week we first moved here."

I did not understand what meetings he was talking about. I had never seen him at any of the Thursday night meetings I had been to, and I did not know of another group of believers in the area. "What meetings?"

"You have been going to the Thursday night youth meetings. The group also has Sunday morning meetings. Every Sunday, your aunt and I get up and go to breakfast and then to the meetings. Your uncle comes with us every other week."

"I didn't know of any other meetings."

"I know. I am sorry, honey. I don't think anyone was intentionally not inviting you to the Sunday meetings, yet they all knew you were my daughter, and they also knew that you didn't know I was a believer. Are you mad?"

I thought about my answer before I said anything. In that moment, I could be my mother's daughter or my father's daughter. I chose to be my father's daughter and choose life over death. "Dad, I forgive you. I know you love me, and I know you too can make mistakes. So far in this life, I have found that I'm not perfect, so how could I expect you to be? Then there's the fact that I've lost a relationship with one parent, and I don't think I could stand to lose you too."

My dad threw his arms around me, crying profusely. "Thank you, honey. I love you."

I thought he was all out of surprises when the doorbell rang. Dad's eyes shot wide open, and he went white as a sheet.

"Who is it, Dad?"

"That would be Elizabeth. I mean Ms. Gilpin."

"You invited her over? Why?"

Before he could answer, my Aunt Marge took hold of Rawdy's hand and told him it was time they left. Dad went to answer the door while Rawdy and I said goodbye. He and I were forever bound together by our experience that day. After they had left, Dad and Ms. Gilpin sat down on the couch. I felt very awkward, so I sat across from them on the loveseat.

Dad took hold of Ms. Gilpin's hand and got this silly grin on his face. "Ruthy, I need to tell you one more thing. I don't apologize for keeping *this* from you because I didn't want to bring Elizabeth into your life until I knew we had a future together.

"You have a future together?"

"I met Elizabeth that very first meeting I went to, after her father prayed for life to return to my body. She was one of the people who kept my name and your aunt's before God. When we moved here, we started talking, and my feelings grew in affection for her, but it wasn't until the Pumpkin Fest that I told her of my feelings." His grin grew larger as he said, "She told me that she also had feelings for me, so I asked her on a date. We have been dating ever since. When I knew that we both wanted more from the relationship, I asked her to spend some time with you and get to know you better. She was completely amazed by you yesterday, and we were both pleased that you could get along with each other amazingly well. So, I felt it was time to tell you."

"You have a future together?"

Dad snorted and nervously chuckled, then replied, "Honey, we would like your permission to marry."

13

The Engagement

I could hardly believe my ears. My dad wanted my permission to marry a woman, a woman who was not my mother. "Really? You want my permission?"

It was Elizabeth that responded this time. "Yes, Ruthy. We want to know you're okay with us getting married. We know this involves you too."

"Wow! This is just such a shock. I had no clue you were dating, let alone ready to get married, and then there's the fact that you just told me you were a believer less than an hour ago. Can I have some time to think about all of this?"

"Sure, honey, take your time. We don't want to rush you."

I left my dad and Elizabeth sitting in the living room and headed to my room for solace. Today I had reached one of the highest highs this world could hold, witnessing one of the most amazing things anyone could imagine, and in that same day my world had just come crashing down once again. I always prided myself on my ability to see the world for how it really was. I was not looking for the fluff of life, the ribbons and bows; I do not even eat the icing off a piece of cake unless I also eat the piece of cake. I thought I knew my dad. He was a man I thought would never sneak around behind my back, but he did, and here I was blindsided once again by a person I thought I knew. I had not felt so alone since my mother told me she was leaving.

My mother's leaving had left a tremendous hole in me. Dad tried as hard as he could to make things right, but he had not made my hole, and he could not fill it either. The divorce was hard, and it had left me with scars, but the lack of a relationship with my own mother did so much more, especially since she did not try to keep any kind of contact. This was the first time that I had allowed myself to think about her leaving me. It had always been too painful, and nothing would be solved by pondering the situation, but I found myself at yet another cross-road. I knew that I must deal with my mother's leaving or be pulverized by the impending future of Elizabeth and my dad.

The controversy inside of me was tearing me apart. My heart started to break, because as much as I might ramble on about my dad doing things behind my back, I was really glad he was a believer. That one little fact made my life easier. The root of all my rambling had more to do with Elizabeth being added to our little happy family than anything else. When Mom left, it was just my dad and I. And even though he was not able to mentally or emotionally help me through the pain, he was still physically there for me every minute of the day, but with someone else in the picture, he would have to divide his attention. Oh, and then there is Elizabeth's child, the promised Gilpin, the anointed child. Could I handle seeing my dad love another child? I had no idea what this "anointed child" would do, but how could little old me compete with someone specially chosen by God? Sure, I knew the figure said that God had a destiny for me, but could that compare to being "anointed" by God?

The hours poured by and so did my tears. I am not sure when I fell asleep, but the sunlight came streaming into my room, and I rolled over to see the clock. My heart started pounding, and panic struck me. It was seven o'clock on Monday morning! I was late to school. I grabbed some clothes off a chair and ran downstairs. When I got out of the bathroom, I noticed that my dad was sitting in the kitchen talking with Dan.

"Dan, what are you doing here?"

"Well, good morning to you too," Dan said with a sarcastic tone.

My dad walked over to me and kissed me on the forehead. "Good morning, honey."

"How come no one woke me up sooner?"

"Ruthy, have you looked outside?"

"No, Dan, but the sun did wake me up this morning. Why?"

"Because if you had looked outside, you would have seen that there are six inches of snow on the ground. School has been canceled for the day."

"Awesome! But you still haven't answered my question. What are you doing here?"

My dad answered my question by saying, "He came back over last night to talk with you, but since you were upstairs in bed, he and I started talking. Close to midnight we ended our discussion, and he was headed out the door to go home, but when I looked outside, I saw four inches of snow and demanded that he spend the night."

"So here I am!" Dan was sitting on a bar stool, spinning around, looking like a kindergartner, screaming, "Whee!"

I went over and gave him a big hug. "I'm glad you're here. So what are we going to do with our day off?"

"We can do whatever you want," Dan explained with his honed diplomatic skills.

I grabbed his hand and pulled him out of the chair. "Let's go outside and make an igloo."

We raced to the door laughing all the way. It was the perfect snow day. After our toes were frozen, we decided it was time to go inside, and so we settled into the living room to watch a movie. The fire was roaring, and we were snuggled under a blanket on the couch. We both had a cup of Dad's famous hot chocolate. It consisted of sixteen ounces of farm fresh milk, six tablespoons of farm fresh cream, and then a combination of milk chocolate chips, bittersweet chocolate chips, and white chocolate chips slowly mixing on a low heat. As the chocolate melts, Dad slowly stirs, making sure the milk does not scald, and nothing burns or sticks to the bottom of the pan. When it is just right, he grabs two large mugs and puts five mini marshmallows in each cup and pours the hot liquid over the top of them.

I could not have asked for a more perfect day, but then at six o'clock it happened. Dad called us into the kitchen for dinner, and I realized that it was the night of Monday Night Football. He had changed his mind, and instead of salmon, he made his famous apricot glazed chicken wings with wasabi dip and fresh vegetables. When that annoying song came on the television, I knew my perfect day was over. I had been replaced by the Kansas City Chiefs.

I never enjoy watching sports, but because Dan was here in my house, I stayed to watch the game. They both said that it was one of the best games they had seen in a while. I would not know why. After the game was over, Dan gave me a hug goodbye and told me he would see me tomorrow. Dad let him out of the house and gave him a pat on the back, right between his shoulder blades, thanking him for coming over. I knew they had bonded, and we were headed in the right direction.

Bright and early Tuesday morning, a car drove up to my house and honked. I peered out my window and saw Rawdy's car. By the time I got downstairs, Sarah was at the front door.

"Are you ready, Ruthy?"

"I'm sorry, Sarah. I'm late as usual. Do I have time to snag some breakfast?"

Sarah turned to look out the window at Rawdy and said, "Rawdy would like to get some coffee from the Coffee Hut. They also have fresh pastries and donuts. Could you get some breakfast there?"

The Coffee Hut is famous for their pastries, and I love their cream cheese Danish pastry with raspberry jelly. "That sounds like a wonderful idea. Let me just grab my things, and I'll be right out."

Aunt Marge had called Dad Monday afternoon to announce the recent courtship between Rawdy and Sarah. So I was not surprised to see Sarah in Rawdy's car Tuesday morning, nor was I surprised that Rawdy was the one driving. He did not like to ride with anyone, let alone a girl. Rawdy seemed happier than usual and was pleased to see me. Sarah climbed into the back seat, relinquishing her dibs on the front seat next to Rawdy. Sarah was beaming from ear to ear. It was evident that Sarah had no lack of confidence that Rawdy would be close to her from now on. I climbed in the car, and we were off. It was evident that Rawdy was different, and I made mention of it to him.

"You have such a peace to you, like you finally fit in your skin."

Rawdy laughed and said, "I wouldn't have put it that way, but you are right. I do feel like I finally fit, as if everything is in place." He glanced back at Sarah and asked, "I guess you've heard the news?"

"Yes, of course. Your mom must have called Dad as soon as you left the room."

Sarah and Rawdy both erupted with laughter, and Rawdy said, "No, we hadn't left the room. Mom grabbed her cell phone as soon as we told them. We heard her entire conversation with your dad, which was filled with lots of screams and tears."

"What are your plans?"

Sarah answered my question. "Rawdy will graduate this year and even though I'm a junior, I only lack a couple credits from graduating myself. We are confident that I can take a couple summer school classes and satisfy the schools requirements. We want to get married in August."

"August! So soon?"

Rawdy glared at me out of the corner of his eye while saying, "Ruthy, not you too. We thought you'd understand and support us."

"Rawdy, I do support you and Sarah, but don't you think you should have a job and a house first?"

Sarah leaned forward and replied, "My grandmother died two months ago, leaving half of her estate to me and half to my parents. I get her house with twenty acres and half of her stocks and bonds. My mom and dad get two hundred acres and the other half of her stocks and bonds. Ruthy, we will both be able to go to college and not have to work."

"Wow! Well, I guess you have it all worked out."

Rawdy put his right hand on my arm and said, "We want this marriage to work, and Sarah is in a position where money will not be an issue for us, but we still want to get a college education. Please, Ruthy. I need you to support me on this."

"Rawdy, of course I will support you and Sarah. I'm just really surprised how this has all worked out. I'm also surprised that you guys are talking about marriage without dating."

"I have always loved Rawdy."

"I know that, Sarah. I don't doubt your feelings or your motives."

Just then we reached our destination, and Rawdy pulled into a parking space. He turned his body toward me and said, "Then what's the issue?"

I was hesitant to share my thoughts, but I knew Rawdy well enough to know he would never leave the car without an answer. "How do the two of you know if you really want to marry each other if you've never even dated? I know that Sarah has never dated anyone, so how is she supposed to know if you are the right one? I know she loves you, but what if..."

I could not say the words that were burning in my throat. I did not have to, Rawdy said them for me. "How do we know we won't end up like your mom and dad? Because God is in this relationship, and we are not going into this blinded by lust. Ruthy, I have known Sarah practically all my life. We were lab partners, played kick ball, picked up trash with the honor society, and we worked side-by-side building a house for Habitat for Humanity."

At that point, Sarah jumped in the conversation. "When I was twelve years old, I was ice skating on Jones pond when the ice broke and I fell through. Rawdy pulled me out and carried me all the way home. Every day for a week after, he came by my house with my homework and helped me study until I got over pneumonia."

Rawdy interjected, "Sarah came over to my house every day for a month when I broke my right arm. She brought my homework and was given permission to fill out my homework until I was able to master writing left-handed."

Sarah started to interrupt Rawdy, but I put up my hand and said, "Okay. I get the point. You have both seen each other at your worst, and you have both selflessly sacrificed for each other, and not just for a year or two, but for most of your life. But how do you know it will last?"

Rawdy picked up both of my hands and with tears in his eyes, he said, "I would die for Sarah, and that is just what I plan on doing for the rest of my life."

"What do you mean?"

"When you love someone, you sacrifice your wants and desires for them, and they do the same for you. With God in our marriage, we both want to live for God's desires and not our own."

"Rawden Jefferson, how do you know so much, being such a new believer?"

Rawdy laughed and gave me a big hug. "I didn't know it at the time, but my mom's been teaching these principles to me for the past two years. I just thought she was trying to do her motherly thing, preparing me for manhood. She never mentioned God, but when I became a believer, it all fit into place, and it was as if I had a CD of my mom's voice playing in my head. For the past two days I've hardly slept. Sarah and I were together most of Monday, and we were talking with our parents the rest of the time."

I was taken back by his grasp of God's teachings and by the love of his mother. I felt a cold, wet drop hit my exposed neck. I was crying.

"Ruthy, are you really this upset over our courtship? We'll have almost eight months before the wedding day, and we'll be going to pre-marriage counseling. It's not as if we haven't known each other our entire life." He paused, waiting for me to answer, but when I didn't he asked, "What's wrong?"

I tried to speak, but I was never able to cry and talk at the same time. Before I could form the words, Sarah spoke. "I think I'm going to go order some coffee and let the two of you talk."

Rawdy gently turned and held me in his arms. "It's okay, Ruthy. I'll always be here for you."

"I know that."

After a few moments of silence, Rawdy said, "So, what's the problem?"

"I know...now I'll always be able to talk to you, but when you get married, Sarah will come first, and when Dad gets married, Elizabeth will come first."

I turned and looked at Rawdy's face. The look in his eyes said more than words could describe.

"Oh, so this is about your mom. I know this whole thing has been hard for you, but you are almost out of school, and your dad deserves to be happy again. I know they would wait to get married, at least until you are done with high school, if that would help you."

It always shocks me when Rawdy pin points the core of a problem. Most people would have gotten caught up on the whole marriage situation, but not Rawdy. He can always see right to the root of a problem. It is uncanny. I sank back into his arms and gazed out the passenger side window. It was nice to be in his arms. I felt safe there, but I did not really want to talk about my mother. I noticed a hawk circling in a thermal wind. He was going around and around, and with each revolution he was climbing higher and higher. I wished I could be like that bird. Freedom.

"So, am I right?"

"Yeah. But I think I could be ninety years old, living in a rest home, and it would still feel the same. She's not...my mom, and what about her anointed child? Have you ever seen this kid?"

"Oh, she's told you about her anointed child. No, of course I haven't seen the child..."

Before he could finish, I interrupted saying, "Has anyone ever seen this child? Maybe it doesn't even exist."

"Well, not yet, because she doesn't have any children."

I was taken back by this latest revelation. I had been sure that Elizabeth told me she had a child. Was I wrong? I pushed out of Rawdy's arms to get a better look at his face. I wanted to be sure he was serious.

"What do you mean?"

It was evident by the look on his face and the tone of his voice that he was getting agitated with me. "I mean...she's never had any children. Her special child is just a prophetic word. That word has been passed down for generations. It might not even happen."

He hesitated, and a smirk formed across his face. Then he said, "Huh...I guess that means your dad might be the father of this special child."

All the emotions came flooding back, and I began to cry again. I was able to squeak out a few words saying, "How can I compete with an anointed child . . . one that is my dad's own flesh and blood?"

At that point, Rawdy was more annoyed with me than concerned, snapping, "Why would you have to compete with a baby?"

"For their attention and affection, you knuckle head."

Rawdy was obviously amused with my frustration, responding, "You don't have to worry about that. Both your father and Elizabeth care deeply for you, and I know your dad will never stop loving you."

I was silent for a moment then said, "My mom did."

Rawdy grabbed me, pulling me closer and with more intensity than he had before, even going as far as to rock me in his arms. "Oh, Ruthy, I don't know if I should be the one to tell you this, but someone should. Your mom wanted to take you with her."

"What?"

I was not sure if it was shock or Rawdy's strangle hold on me, but either way I could not breathe. I had to free myself from his arms, yet I resisted the desire to hop out of the car and run. I felt so uncomfortable, not even knowing how to sit still. I stared down at my fingernails and picked at the pink polish. How could Rawdy say such horrible things about the only person that I could honestly say I knew truly loved me? How could my dad keep me from my mom? Why would Dad do such a thing? My mind kept telling me to open the door and just run for it. The only thing that kept me in the car was the intense desire to know why he would say such a thing. I had to get a grip on myself, so that is what I did. I wrapped my arms around my chest and grabbed my shoulders, burying my chin.

"Rawdy, why would my dad do such a thing?"

Rawdy grabbed the steering wheel, twisting his hands back and forth, looking at some place in the distance. "One night I overheard my mom tell my dad that it was your dad who refused to let your mother take you. He wanted you to be raised as a believer, and since she wasn't a believer, he wouldn't let her take you."

Surprisingly, I wasn't shocked. How could I be mad at my dad for wanting me to be a believer? Yet the loss of my mother had done inoperable damage to my emotions and heart, and in the end, my mother should have fought harder to keep me, no matter what.

"I heard something like that once, but it doesn't change the fact that she traded me for half the farm. What kind of love is that?"

"Well, I don't know the entire situation, but I know she hit your dad with a plunger, left him with that scar over his right eye, and your dad threatened to go to the police with charges of spousal abuse if she tried to fight him for custody. What choice did she have?"

"So you're trying to tell me that my mom fought to keep me, but my dad threatened her, so she gave up?"

"I guess you're right that your dad bought her off with the farm money, but that was to get her to promise not to try and contact you until you were eighteen."

I had to let go of the grip I had on myself. I was now the one cutting off my circulation.

"What? Wait a minute. Why eighteen?"

"You'd be an adult and could choose for yourself."

His words hit heavy on my heart. It was only a little over a year until I turned eighteen. Would my mother try to find me, or would she just forget that I existed? Not another word was spoken until Sarah came back to the car. She had three coffees, my cheese Danish, and a doughnut for Rawdy.

Sarah handed us our coffees and pastry and finally broke our deafening silence. Unaware of our recent conversation, she exclaimed, "We are not engaged yet, we are just courting."

Neither Rawdy nor I said a word. I enjoyed the Danish, but not as much as I thought I would. My thoughts were weighing on my stomach, causing it to churn. I was not sure if Sarah was telling me the truth or just trying to make me feel better. Honestly, I did not know what the difference between courting and being engaged was when the ultimate conclusion to both is marriage. Rawdy had given me much to think about, and yet nothing had changed. My mother had still abandoned me and had taken money meant to buy her off. My feelings for my mother had not changed. I was still mad at her, and I had only been surprised that Rawdy and Sarah would be getting married so soon. I knew the moment Rawdy became a believer that he would marry Sarah one day. But there had been information revealed that once again had my head spinning, and there was no way to make it stop. Was Rawdy correct in assuming that Elizabeth did not have any children at this time? Or was he mistaken, and she had given birth to a child in secret?

14

History of a Town

I held off giving Elizabeth and Dad an answer for two weeks. Every morning I could tell my dad was hoping for an answer, but I was not going to give them an answer just to satisfy them. This decision did involve me, even though I did not believe I had a right to tell them they could or could not get married. I decided I was not going to take this responsibility lightly. They had asked me a question, and I did a lot of soul searching for the answer. I was still not positive if Elizabeth had a child, but I had come to the conclusion that I could not stand in the way of my dad's happiness. I was still not sure how I felt about the fact that Dad had told mom to stay out of my life. I was not happy about it, but I was mentally and emotionally exhausted. I could not afford to be angry with my dad.

Dad and I started going to the gatherings together on Sunday mornings, along with Aunt Marge, Uncle Rick, Rawdy, and Elizabeth–she would sit next to Dad. I knew I had to give them my answer soon. So I tested my dad, asking him if the three of us could meet on Monday night to discuss their possible marriage, knowing that Monday night was a big game for his favorite team. He did not hesitate or blink an eye when he answered, he simply said, "Okay." I knew then he was in love, and she was more important to him than his big screen TV, recliner, or the Kansas

City Chiefs. Secretly, I hoped she would never be more important to him than me.

Elizabeth was right on time for dinner, scoring points with my dad, dressed in a classic, black, tea length dress. With her three inch heels, she stood head to head with Dad. I was watching them, imagining the wedding day. They would make a beautiful couple. My dad was even looking younger; he gained close to ten pounds the last couple months, plumping out most of his wrinkles. Dad's skin color had faded to a warm shade of ivory, removing five years instantly. He had even gone to the dentist and had his teeth whitened.

My dad once again had created a masterpiece meal consisting of poached salmon, steamed baby carrots, dinner rolls, and a homemade chocolate meringue pie. That was why he saved the salmon. I enjoyed seeing Elizabeth eat Dad's meal. She ate everything he put on her plate, and she asked for seconds. To my dad, eating his meal is as good as saying you love him.

I drug out the evening as long as I could. It would be the last time in their relationship that I would have the upper hand. It was not really the better side of my character, but I justified it to myself because I was soon going to make them the two happiest people in Gilpinton.

We settled into the living room with Dad and Elizabeth on the couch and me in Dad's recliner. I knew it would not be long until Dad was back to sitting in his recliner. I was taking advantage of every opportunity. I had prepared for this evening all week long, yet I still seemed to be in a lack for words, and I continued to fight the fear of being alone.

"Elizabeth...Dad...I've asked you two here tonight to give you my decision." I was sitting up straight on the edge of the chair, taking deep breaths between each name–only for drama's sake. Both of their faces looked quite intense. I doubt they knew for sure what my answer would be, but of course, I knew there was only one answer I could give.

"I want to thank both of you for giving me this opportunity. It really means a lot to me that you would care so much about my feelings." I cleared my throat, and a smile broke out across my face. I caught the gaze of my dad, and my ruse was over. "I can't keep this up any longer. Of course I'll give you my blessing. I'm so excited about the two of you getting married."

Dad leaped across the room, scooping me up out of the chair and swinging me around the room. When he put me down, Elizabeth grabbed me and hugged as tightly as she could. We all had tears in our eyes, and the smiles plastered across our faces could not be any wider.

I was excited to have a woman back in our house, but I still had a nagging fear that I would be on the outside looking in on this happy family. I still did not know if Elizabeth had a child, but the idea kept tormenting me, so I was determined to get to the bottom of the mystery tonight.

"Elizabeth, you once mentioned something about your child, and I was wondering, since we're going to be a family now, when can I meet your kid?"

Dad looked at Elizabeth with confusion and fear. His mouth was wide open, but no sound was being made. Elizabeth had a similar look of shock and was struggling to get her words out. "I... I...I...I don't have a kid." She paused to catch her breath. "I was speaking of a prophesied child that I might have in the future. There is no possible way I could have a child yet."

Dad finally found his voice and exclaimed, "You have a child?" He obviously had not been listening to Elizabeth. "What is Ruthy talking about, and why have you never told me?"

Elizabeth laughed and said, "No, I've never been married, nor have I ever been pregnant. I told Ruthy about the prophetic word that was given to my great-great-great-grandfather which said my generation would have a child anointed by God to do amazing things. And since I am the last of the descendents of Carl Gilpin II, it will fall to my child to fulfill the prophesy he was given. It has been prophesied that the sixth generation will give birth to a child who will bring the knowledge of Jesus to the entire town of Gilpinton."

"Was he the founder of Gilpinton?"

"Well, actually he was the founder, but he named the town after his first cousin, William Gilpin, who encouraged much of the westward expansion. He was also a believer and was raised in a gathering referred to as the Religious Society of Friends. William came from a very wealthy family and studied in England. He wanted to name a city after his family in the Kansas City area, but the idea was rejected. My great-great-great grandfather, Carl Gilpin II, decided to honor him by naming this little town after him, and the rest is history. William was quoted as saying, 'Progress is God.' His gathering was known for pushing for the end of slavery, women's rights, and other social issues of the day."

Elizabeth paused for a moment and went to the kitchen, grabbing three glasses of sweet ice tea. I seized the opportunity to inquire about the prophetic word concerning her anointed child.

"Elizabeth, so who received the prophesy, Carl or William?"

Elizabeth handed each of us a glass and sat back down next to my dad responding, "I know it's all a bit confusing, but it's pretty simple. My great-great-great grandfather, Carl Gilpin II, on my father's side, was a believer and a leader of a gathering in Smithton, Missouri. His church was well known for miracles and great teachings. After he'd been a teacher for seven years, he received direction from God to move to the countryside near Kingdom City, Missouri. He went looking for a plot of land he could purchase and found a three hundred acre farm. The kitchen of my parent's house sits on the foundation of his original house.

"When Carl was in his late fifties, he built a much larger house which is now the city library. Carl built a meeting hall and started having gatherings. People were extremely amazed by his speech, and many people were being healed. He soon purchased more land and built a boarding house. After a couple years, Carl purchased more land and soon owned five square miles of property. He sold plots of land, and people began to build houses, stores, and even a school. They started calling it Gilpintown, but it wasn't an official town. Finally, after twenty years, Carl worked to create a state recognized township. Most of the people thought he should just go ahead and name the town Gilpintown, but Carl wanted to pay homage to his famous relative, William Gilpin, so he decided to use the name William had desired, Gilpinton.

"Even though the town started as an all believer's town, after several years, non-believers started moving into the town. Carl contracted tuberculosis and died at the age of sixty-three, but before he died, a wise man came to visit him and his gathering. This man was named Benjamin Gorman, and he was known for giving prophetic words to believers. He went to visit Carl on his death bed. He spoke the Word of God over him and asked him if he had any regrets in his life. Carl told Benjamin he was sad to see half of Gilpinton being inhabited by non-believers. He had hoped that the non-believers would turn to God through their interaction with believers–Carl felt it had been his biggest failure.

"Benjamin spoke to God and read the Bible with Carl for three days and nights, never leaving his side. On the morning of the fourth day, Benjamin received a vision from God. Benjamin shared the vision with Carl, and within minutes, Carl was gone. Benjamin wrote the vision down, gave it to Carl's wife, then left. My great-great-great grandfather had three sons and one daughter. Carl and his wife named their oldest son, William Carl Gilpin. He was my great-great grandfather."

My dad was acting as if he was still in shock, yet his face held the expression of understanding. He was coming out of a stupor when he said, "I think I read a quote of his once. Something about Americans should subdue something and go to the Pacific Ocean… change darkness to light…and something about destiny. I've been searching for my destiny. I'm not sure, but I think I even ended up in California trying to reach the Pacific Ocean because of that statement."

Elizabeth responded, "Yes, William Gilpin did say something like that…give or take a few words. He later became the governor of Colorado. My family is very proud of him and wanted to pay homage to his legacy. So to answer, once and for all, your original question, I do *not* have any children…yet."

My dad released a big sigh of relief; you could see the relief on his face, yet the look on Elizabeth's face was growing more intense and disapproving by the minute.

"Eli, don't you want more children?"

The room was filled with tension, and I knew my dad's response could end any hope of a future with Elizabeth with one simple word. What would he say? I never thought that my dad might not want more children. He had been such a great dad, and he loves babies. I just assumed he would be eager to have more children, but there was the small possibility that he thought he was too old to have more children.

I was right.

Dad was relatively quick to answer with a resounding, "I would love to have more kids."

He grabbed Elizabeth about the waist and twirled her around with great enthusiasm; he was even making me dizzy! I expected Dad, or even Elizabeth, to look at me for approval, or at least a sympathetic nod, but they did not. My power was over. From that point on, they would make decisions without seeking my consent, but always consulting each other of course.

The next few days we focused our attention on my car—to my delight. Dad and Rawdy were engrossed in the finer details of restoring a *classic* car, while I was consumed with the anticipation of having my own car. Most of the work was pretty straightforward: take nut off, put nut back on, take off old hose, put on new hose. While other aspects were fairly complicated: turn your elbow ninety degrees and screw the clamp counterclockwise while holding your breath, hoping you do not drop anything into never-to-be-seen-again land. The repairs were difficult as usual. Dad was searching for original style parts, while I was happy with universal ones. The universal were sometimes harder to retrofit, but they were readily available, while the original style took a detective to find.

I never understood why, when men have such large hands, the manufacturing engineers design such small parts and holes for them to go into. My dad always said he needed my help to fix something because I had small hands. Maybe the real reason everything is engineered small is so men cannot do it for themselves and have to ask for help. I believe the underlying scheme is to help every man fulfill his desire to be the foreman, so they can be the one telling someone else what to do.

I did not mind working with my dad or Rawdy, but I had to draw the line when it came time to take out the old heater core. Dad said he just could not do it, and Rawdy was mysteriously absent that day, but to my salvation, Dan showed up just in time. Dad convinced him he could do the job, and his manly ego would not let him quit once he started. Replacing the heater core was the least desirable job. Dan spent most of that Saturday lying at a forty-five degree angle with his feet in the air, knees on the passenger head rest, rear end on seat, and his head under the dash. We finished my car in just under three weeks.

During the last week, on that Saturday, Dad had a little welding to do on the car's frame. Dad worked for a welding shop as a teenager and had never gotten over seeing one man's contacts melt onto his eye balls. The guy had stopped by the welding shop to have a part welded. According to my dad, the man did not have any common sense because he stood right behind Dad without a welding helmet, peeking as he welded the piece back together. You should never watch welding being done without a protective welding helmet! Needless to say, my dad is adamant about no one being any closer than fifty yards from him while he is welding. Even then, he would rather you had your back to him just in case you are tempted to look. When I was a small child, my dad always made sure I was in the house under my mom's close supervision when he welded. And now as a teenager, he sent me off with Elizabeth for the day while he finished welding.

Elizabeth decided to take me shopping for gift favors for their wedding. I had never seen so many different kinds of bubble bottles. They had plain plastic bottles, heart shaped bottles, rose shape bottles, lip shaped bottles, dove shaped bottles, candy-kiss shaped bottles, and all in no less than ten colors. She also had me sample mints to go in small heart shaped tins. There were peppermint mints, spearmint mints, lemon mints, cherry mints, and my favorite: lemon with raspberry center mints. At the end of the day, I was not sure if Elizabeth had decided on any one item, but I was hoping that in the future she would take my dad instead of me.

We arrived back at my house around midnight. We called ahead and told Dad we would be late. He said that he was exhausted and was headed to bed, so Elizabeth dropped me off and went home. It was not until the next morning that I saw my dad. I could not control my laughter; he was a sight to behold. He looked like a lobster, bright red from his neck to his ankles. Saturday had been an unusually warm day, reaching near eighty degrees Fahrenheit. Even though the day was rather warm, the sun was behind clouds the entire day. Dad had taken advantage of the warm weather and put on shorts and a tank-top. That Sunday morning, I found him in the kitchen with ice-packs on both of his thighs. Every area of his body which had not been covered by clothing or his welding helmet was burned. You see, the light emitted from the welder has the same effect on skin as the bright sun. I tried to control my laughter because it was obvious he was in considerable pain. Elizabeth had the same reaction, with a bit more sympathy.

I was ecstatic when I was finally able to drive my car, even though the first several weeks were a bit bumpy. I would like to take a moment to say that my driving skills are impeccable, but with little to no practice, a slight accident should be expected. The road was a little icy, and I must have hit the brakes too hard, because I blew a tire when I ran over the storm drain. Or maybe I should describe it more like: I slammed into the storm drain grate, puncturing the front passenger side tire and bending the rim. It took another two days to find a new rim. Needless to say, my dad was not happy, and it got even worse when the same thing happened to the driver's side front tire the next week on my way home from school.

Dad decided I needed a job, explaining, "Ruth, honey, you will learn the value of a dollar if you expend your energy and time to pay for a new tire, rim, and for your gas."

I was not happy about it at first, but then I chose to see it as an opportunity for independence. Dad said that whatever money I earned was mine to do with as I pleased, that is, as long as the one new tire, rim, and all of my gas were paid first. Thankfully, he was still willing to pay the insurance and taxes. I could hardly complain–most of my friends did not have their own car, and the ones that did were not nearly as impressive as mine.

The first day I drove my car to school, I was mobbed by no less than twenty boys begging to take it for a spin. The following week, I still had close to ten guys pleading just to drive it around the parking lot, and even after a month, there were five guys hopelessly still begging. After I had blown the second tire, most of the male student body had a few choice words for me, all of which circled around my *supposed* inability to drive such an exquisite piece of automotive history. I chose to take the high road and not be offended by their ludicrous remarks.

The next two months went by rather fast–I was concentrating on the preparations for the wedding and my recent employment at the Coffee Hut. I was to be Elizabeth's maid-of-honor, and Uncle Rick would be Dad's best man. They would hold the wedding in Aunt Marge's immaculately landscaped backyard on the first Saturday in June. It would be the talk of this sleepy little town for years to come.

It seemed like I was engulfed by wedding preparations. Rawdy and Sarah were closing in on their wedding date and had finalized most of their arrangements. I was to be one of three bridesmaids, and Dan had been chosen as one of the groomsmen. The closer their wedding day got, the more obvious it was that Rawdy's heart was longing for the companionship of his former friends. Rawdy had personally gone to Chad and Mike, trying to persuade them to join us and become believers, but they would not hear of it. Chad had not said anything to Dan or me for several weeks, but his threat was still very real and active. Unfortunately, Rawdy, following his heartfelt plea to Chad, had been added to Chad's list with Dan and me, an unexpected consequence.

Dan and I were still spending every free moment together, yet our time together dwindled with the addition of my job and Dan's recent decision.

15

Bolt from the Blue

It was late in the month of February when Dan took me aside one Sunday afternoon, revealing a decision that would change both our lives forever.

"I've decided to go on to higher education and become a church leader. I assure you that I want a future with you, but I need to concentrate on my studies without the duties of a husband."

"Really?" I said dumbfounded.

"I'll go to the local community college for two years and get my associates degree. Then I'll need to go another four years for religious studies to become a gathering leader."

"Really?" I was about in tears.

"Ruthy, I hate to make you wait, but it's for the best. I'll need to work hard to pay for my classes and living quarters. I don't think I can handle the pressures of a new marriage on top of all that."

His hand touched my check and wiped a tear. I had been immersed in wedding preparations for not one, but two weddings for almost three months. I had agreed to help Elizabeth bake and decorate Sarah's wedding cake. I was going to be a bridesmaid in both weddings, and I had to sample mints, cakes, punches, and chicken cooked a dozen different ways. I had seen over a hundred different wedding dresses and was going to wear two hideous bridesmaid's gowns. Not to mention the fact that I would be expected to stand, smashed together with twenty or so other single women, in the hopes of *not* catching the wedding bouquet– you can never be sure anymore what the wedding party will do to the girl who catches the bouquet and the guy who catches the garter. I was rejoicing with two immeasurably happy brides-to-be finished with their wedding day plans, only to stand there and have this man, whom I love, tell me that it would be at least another six years until I could plan my own wedding. On top of everything, he still did not want to make anything official between the two of us.

My emotions came flooding out, and I could do nothing to hold them back.

Dan threw me a lifeline and explained that there was another way he could go which would speed up the process. "Ruthy, I could start taking classes on weekends and then this summer, but that will greatly limit our time together. I would like your opinion. If you don't want me to do it, I'll wait. What do you say?"

I sucked back my tears and said, "I think I would rather sacrifice a few hours a week now rather than several years. How much time will you save doing it this way?"

Dan grabbed both of my hands and kissed them.

"If I go every weekend and summer for the next two years, I'll be able to complete it all in three and a half years. Can you...no... will you wait for me?"

Three and a half years rang through my head. Could I wait? Do I want to wait? No...I do not want to wait that long, but do I want to be with Dan forever? Yes, I do. I slowly pulled his hands up to my shoulder height. I laid my cheek on his hands–a tear rolled down and onto his wrist. I picked my head back up and looked into his eyes, then I leaned down again, pursing my lips together, and I kissed the tops of both of his hands, "Yes...I will."

The last week of April was our school's spring break. Dan chose to use the time to get further ahead in his studies, while I used it to grab extra hours at the Coffee Hut. Dan was trying to save every penny he could, so we were driving my car around instead of his. I could not tell him that my dad was making me pay for gas, so I was glad to have the opportunity to make a few extra bucks. That Thursday, Elizabeth went to school to catch up on her lesson plans and was going to stop in at the Coffee Hut before going home. The shop was pretty slow that evening. With the arrival of spring, most of the town was going to the drive-in theater. Elizabeth had put in a long day, arriving at the Coffee Hut only an hour before closing time. I made her a Vanilla Bean Coffee Spin, and she picked out a lemon cheese cake with raspberry sauce.

Since no one was in the store, I grabbed a spin for myself and we talked. She seemed to understand how hard it was for me to rejoice with her and Sarah, and yet have the heartache of at least a three year wait myself. I know I have another year of high school, but I had as many credits as Sarah and could have graduated early too, but Dan and my dad would not hear of it. Elizabeth did not share any sob stories with me, but I was sure she had her share of stories of friends getting married before her.

Elizabeth patted my right hand and said, "You will make it through this. I know it's hard to see that now, but you will."

I was not sure how to respond, so I glanced at the far wall, trying not to catch her gaze. I was startled to see it was fifteen minutes past eight. The Coffee Hut closed at eight, but without other customers distracting me, I had become engulfed in our conversation and lost all track of time. I quickly got up to lock the front door, happy to find a distraction. I had just turned around when I heard a tapping on the glass door.

There were two men standing at the door. They were both strangers to me, and I told them through the closed door that the store was closed. The man pleaded with me to open the door, under the pretense of asking me a question. I looked at Elizabeth for reassurance. She nodded her head in agreement. Something inside of me told me not to open the door, but my nature is one of obedience, so I unlocked the door. Before I could pull the door open, the younger man pushed his way in and grabbed me around my shoulders. He was holding a knife to my throat while the older gentleman proceeded over to Elizabeth and tied her hands behind her back with a zip tie. It was all such a blur, almost like watching a movie, but I was actually living this horror film.

I heard screaming and voices and realized I was the one screaming. The older man slapped me across the face. I could not make out what the voices were saying. It was then that I realized that the dark hole was closing in on me. I was going to faint.

When I came to, I found my hands tied behind my back, and my vision was completely black. I started to scream for Elizabeth. Elizabeth quickly started saying, "Shh...please, Ruthy, keep your voice down. I'm right here."

"Where are we? I can't see anything. What is going to happen to us?"

Elizabeth's voice was slow and deliberate, but I could tell she was afraid. "Your eyes are ok. They have taken us to some old building–there are no windows in this room. I don't know what is going to happen to us."

"Why did they do this? Did they steal money from the store?"

"No, they didn't rob the store. They even locked the door behind us. I can't understand it, but I do believe you'll be just fine."

"Me? What about you?"

"Don't worry. Your dad will come looking for us and see both of our cars at the Coffee Hut, and then he'll get others together to come find us. I heard the two men talking right before you fainted. They weren't going to bring you along, but then a third man came in and told him that I was going to marry your father, and you would become my step-daughter."

"What would that have to do with anything?"

"Ruthy, I think this might have something do to with the Balaamites."

"What is that?"

"They are a group of people who have chosen to follow the way of Balaam. They were all once believers, but they willingly chose to compromise the principles of God and proclaim things contrary to the Word of God. Because they were all once believers in our gathering, they also know about the prophetic word that was given concerning my child. Some of our gathering leaders were concerned something like this might happen."

"Why?"

"Because I will soon be married, and the prophetic word could finally be fulfilled. They want to make sure I don't get married and have a child. I'm afraid you were just in the wrong place at the wrong time, Ruthy. They were after me, and you just happened to be with me."

"What will they do to us, Elizabeth?"

There was a long pause, and I could hear her clearing her throat. She was as scared as I was. She finally composed herself enough to speak.

"Ruthy, I can't say what they intend to do, but I know that God is on our side. We need to ask God for help. Just try to keep your voice down, because we don't want to make them any angrier."

We both started speaking to God, asking Him to send someone to rescue us. I started asking God for another big messenger to come and save us. I could not tell how much time had passed, but it seemed like hours. I must have fallen asleep, because I was unaware of anyone entering the room, but I could hear two men talking and Elizabeth responding to their questions. I still could not see, but I could tell they had moved her because her voice sounded like she was higher than floor level, either sitting or standing. We had both been lying on the floor. I kept very still, pretending to still be sleeping. Most of the conversation was undistinguishable, but I did hear her say my name and plead with the men to let me go.

One of the men said, "She may very well be the so-called 'anointed child'. We will do no such thing."

I heard Elizabeth say, "There is no way she could be the anointed child. She is not a blood heir. Just let her go."

I was gripped by a sudden urge to vomit. How could I be the anointed child? Even if neither Elizabeth nor I believed I was, I was not safe if these Balaamites believed I could be. What were they going to do to me?

After a short time, I heard footsteps, and the room grew quiet. Elizabeth started speaking to God with great intensity.

"Elizabeth, are they going to kill us?"

Elizabeth had tried to conceal her fear from me earlier, but now she was obviously raw with emotion from her recent ordeal and was unable to speak without crying.

"Ruthy, I don't know what is going to happen. We must ask God to send us a way out, and fast." I knew she was right.

I had recently come to know God's amazing power and abilities, but I also knew that Dan died once, and even though in the end he was raised from the dead, he told me he still remembered the pain of that death. Would there be a miracle, and someway we would escape this nightmare, or would we be killed and miraculously be brought back from the dead too? Dan had passionately expressed his concern for me, and his desire to keep me from a fate such as his. Could I bear to live with the memory of my tragic death for the rest of my living life? Under my breath I said, "Lord, I hope not."

Suddenly, a man crashed through the door and turned on a light. Hot bile crept up my throat. I reached for Elizabeth. For the first time, I could see the dungeon they had entombed us in. It was a twenty by twenty foot room with a small sink and a toilet. A single chair sat in the far corner of the room. There were no windows, and the light was an old florescent light fixture that only had one working light tube. The other tube kept flickering but never came on. The entire room was covered with old boards, and the door was one you might find in an old barn. The man gave us each a glass of water and a cheese sandwich, but he did not say anything to either of us. He just stood there watching us eat. As soon as we were done, he took the sandwich wrappers and empty water glasses and left the room. This was also the first time I had a chance to get a good look at Elizabeth. Her hair was covered in blood, and her lip was swollen and busted open.

"What did they do to you?"

Elizabeth gingerly looked at me and cried. I could see that she was genuinely scared. I put myself in her shoes and realized even a woman of great faith, such as Elizabeth, would be concerned not only with the immediate danger, but also with the opinion of my dad. What will he do after all of this is over, assuming we get out of this alive. Will he blame her for putting me in this position? Is he blaming himself right now? I am his little girl, and he has sacrificed a lot for me. Will he still want to marry her?

"Ruthy, I'm so sorry. This is entirely my fault."

"Elizabeth, this is not your fault. You had nothing to do with this or the prophesy."

I knew I had to say something to reassure her, but what more could I say? Before I knew what I was saying, the words were coming out of my mouth.

"The men don't want to kill us. They just wanted to keep you from marrying my dad. By now my dad knows something is wrong, and he'll be here soon. I'm sure of it."

My words seemed to calm Elizabeth, and I was hoping that somehow they had been inspired words.

Three more times the man came into the room and brought us cheese sandwiches and water. Neither Elizabeth nor I could tell how many hours were between each visit, but we knew it had to be close to six hours. We fell in and out of sleep, but without daylight or a clock, we were unable to grasp the length of time we had been held in captivity.

The next thing we knew, three men entered the room. The big guy grabbed Elizabeth while the younger guy held me down. They took her away and left me in the room screaming for her. I was alone. I was scared. The room was completely silent, and time seemed to stand still. I had no concept of how long I was there alone, but the next voice I heard was that of my dad.

"Ruthy, oh my Ruthy! You're okay!"

Dad scooped me up into his arms, holding me close to his chest.

"Oh, Daddy!"

"It's okay, honey, you're safe now. No one is going to hurt you."

Panic rang out in my voice as I said, "Where's Elizabeth? Is she okay?"

"Don't worry about her. She'll be fine. They've taken her to the hospital."

A tall skinny man in scrubs came into the room. He started poking on me and took my temperature. He then said, "We need to start an IV right away. She is dehydrated, but overall I think she'll be fine."

"Daddy, did they hurt Elizabeth?"

"Not really. She has a couple broken bones in her face, and she has a stab wound, but nothing fatal."

"Not really!? They stabbed her?"

"We found her right as he was going to stab her, but we weren't able to get to her in time. It took us another two days to find you."

"Two days! How long have I been here?"

"You've been gone for a total of four days, sweetheart."

I could hardly believe it. It turned out our captors had only fed us once a day, so each cheese sandwich was the marking of a new day. The last two days I had been without food, and the only water I had was what I was able to drink out of the small sink's faucet.

"We need to get you checked out at the hospital. You can see Elizabeth there."

Dad proceeded to fill me in on all the details during the drive to the hospital. When Elizabeth did not answer her phone Thursday at nine o'clock, Dad went looking for both of us. He found our cars at the Coffee Hut and found Elizabeth's engagement ring on the sidewalk outside the door. Elizabeth had slipped it off knowing that my dad would suspect something was wrong if he found her ring. He called the leaders of our gathering, and they called the police. It turns out that Chad's father was a leader of the Balaamites, and was irate over Rawdy trying to convert Chad, so much so that he felt he had to take action. The Balaamites believed if they could stop Elizabeth from marrying my dad, then she would not have a child, at least not for a few years. They followed her to the Coffee Hut, waiting for her to come out. Dad did not think they meant to take me, but Chad's father came in and saw I was there, and knowing I was Eli's daughter, he demanded they bring me along.

The gathering divided into two groups, half speaking requests to God and half searching. Dan spent the first day searching, but then he locked himself in his bedroom, speaking to God and fasting–only coming out for water and bathroom breaks. After three days, he emerged from his room with specific directions where they would find Elizabeth. He had fallen asleep. Although he did not know where to find me, he had a dream of Elizabeth's location. They found Elizabeth right where he told them to look. Chad's father had taken Elizabeth two miles east of the building they had been hiding us in. For some unknown reason, Chad's father had stopped on an old gravel road and was going to kill Elizabeth there.

Dan spent another day seeking God's wisdom and requesting my safe return while the rest were still out searching. Finally, Dan knew I was in an old barn on Lambert Road, but he did not know they had me in a hidden room under the floor of the old barn. They sent word back to Dan, letting him know that I was not there, and after two more hours of speaking to God, he was able to tell them where to find the hidden door.

As we arrived at the hospital, my pain killers were taking effect, and I was completely out of it. Several hours later I awoke screaming for help.

"Ruthy, I'm here. Shh...it's ok," Dan softly said.

"Dan...oh...Dan!" I was unable to stop crying or trembling.

"Are you ok? Should I get help?"

"I had a bad dream. I was all alone back in that room. No one could find me, and no one could hear me. I was able to hear my dad's voice coming from outside, but I could not make him hear me."

Dan put his arms around me. "Shh...Ruthy, you're safe now. You're in the hospital. No one is going to hurt you now. Your dad went to get a drink, but he'll be back soon. Should I go get him?"

I was groggy from the medicine, but was still able to manage some form of composure. I pushed him away from me exclaiming, "No! I'm fine. It was just a dream and...the effects of...the medicine. I'm glad to see you."

I leaned over and gave him a big hug.

"You don't know how glad I am to see you. I...I don't know what I would have done if..."

"Shh...don't say it. I know what you're thinking, and I don't want those thoughts in your head ever again. I'm fine, Dan. They didn't hurt me."

He sat down on my hospital bed and took a hold of my left hand.

"Ruthy, I have to go."

"Well, I'm sure it's late. You should be home in bed right now. What time is it anyway?"

"It's midnight, but that's not what I mean. I have to go away for a while."

"What? No, I haven't seen you for days. And what could be so important that you have to leave me now?"

"The General Council of Gatherings needs to be briefed on what has happened to you and Elizabeth, and I'm the delegate for our area."

Tears welled up in my eyes, and I started to quiver. He took a hold of my hand. "This is very important. I have to go."

Gingerly, I said, "I don't want you to leave."

"Oh, Ruthy, please don't make this harder than it already is. The thought of leaving you is tearing me apart, but I have no choice. The Balaamites will soon learn that Eli and Elizabeth are still going to marry. Then they will try something else, and if..."

Dan abruptly stopped in mid-sentence. Concern was written all over his face. He was looking down at the linoleum floor, but his mind was obviously a million miles away.

"Dan, what is it? What aren't you telling me?"

As a matter of fact he stated, "Nothing. Everything's fine. Everything will be just fine. I have to go and meet with the council. I'll be back within a week, and I'll call you the first chance I get."

"When will that be?"

"I might not be able to call for a couple days, but as soon as I can, I will. I promise."

I sat up in bed and wrapped my arms around Dan. I did not want to let go, but he pulled my arms away and took both of my hands in his. He looked me straight in the eye and said, "Ruthy, I've spent the last four days and nights seeking God's wisdom and requesting your safe return. I did that for you." He looked away for a second, then said, "Well, maybe for me, too. I've never thought about any girl for that length of time. I couldn't sleep, and I couldn't eat. My point is...I need you in my life. I want you in my life *forever*."

He took my right hand and kissed it, and then he lifted my left hand and kissed it.

"I can't make a commitment to you yet. I still have three years until my schooling is complete, but I do hope you will wait for me."

My heart was pounding, and my palms were practically dripping wet. He had just made me so happy, but I could feel the black sheet from the medication overtaking me again, and I knew I had to answer him while I still could.

"I'll wait for you as long...as I have to."

Dan quickly leaned forward and kissed me on the forehead. I slumped back into the bed and started drifting to sleep.

"Ruthy, I have to leave now. I'll call you as soon as I can."

Over and over I heard Sarah's voice saying, "Love is an action." I knew what I had to say. "Dan?"

"Yeah."

"I love you too." I could have sworn I faintly heard him answer me back, but I am not sure because I was unconscious before I finished my own sentence.

The next morning I awoke to find my dad sitting by my side, sleeping. The nurse was taking my blood pressure and checking my vitals. She followed my gaze to my dad and said, "He hasn't left your side."

I looked at the clock. It was still early morning.

"Elizabeth," I exclaimed.

"No, dear, my name is Nancy." The polite older nurse looked at me with pity.

Dad was sitting by my side. Sadness filled my heart, and I had to see Elizabeth.

"Can I get up? I want to go see Elizabeth."

"Sure. You'll be going home today. Let me help you out of bed."

She helped me off the side of the bed, into a robe, and directed me to Elizabeth's room. Elizabeth had several stitches in her face and was pretty bruised, but a rather large smile was plastered across her face.

"Ruthy, it's good to see you."

I rushed over to her and gave her a bear hug, and we both started crying. When we finally composed ourselves, Elizabeth asked, "How is your father?"

"Hasn't he come to see you?"

"Ruthy, he's been worried about you, his little girl. I wouldn't expect him to come to me until he knew you were okay."

"Well, I would. I can't believe he hasn't seen you. He is sleeping in my room right now. I'll go get him."

"No!" She composed herself and calmly said, "No, don't bother him. Let him sleep. I can't imagine he's gotten much sleep these last four days."

"Four days. I still can't believe it was that long."

"Me either, but it was."

Before we could say another word, my dad entered the room, but he seemed strange, and he never approached Elizabeth.

Elizabeth ended the awkward silence, "Hi, Eli."

"Hello, Elizabeth. How are you feeling?"

"Much better today. The doctor says I'll be able to go home today."

"Me too," I interjected.

Dad said, "The gathering is going to have a lunch in your honor. Everyone wants to see you. That is if you are both up to such a thing."

"I think that sounds nice. How about you, Ruthy?"

I looked up at my dad, trying to get a sense of his emotions, and answered, "I think a dinner would be great. I'm starved for some good food."

Dad and Elizabeth both laughed, and then Dad said, "I think I'll go and find out what time you can get out of here, Ruthy."

Dad left the room, leaving Elizabeth and I alone. Had she noticed that he did not mention her name? I took the opportunity to question Elizabeth on a few details.

"What did they do to you?" She was hesitant to answer, but I persisted. "Please!"

"After they took me from that room, they started arguing about killing us. I tried to talk them into leaving you alone, but they just smacked me across the face with the butt end of a pistol." Her face grimaced with an obvious memory of the event. "Two of the men decided to leave, saying, 'I don't want anything to do with this.' Lee, Chad's father, started yelling at me. None of what he said made sense. He was speaking English, but he was obviously a disturbed man. He heard a vehicle coming down the driveway, so he put the gun to my head and pulled the trigger."

I gasped loudly, causing Elizabeth to glance up at me. She gave me a slight smile with tears in her eyes. Then she resumed the story. "The gun didn't fire. He threw down the gun and pulled out a large hunting knife and held it to my throat. I felt a burning sensation as he drew the knife across my neck, but there's no mark of that happening. Lee put me in his car and drove for a couple miles then pulled me out.

"Lee was standing behind me, holding my head back, when he raised his right hand. I noticed a car drive up the road and watched as Eli got out. It seemed like it was in slow motion. My mind was racing."

"I bet so."

"Yeah. As your father was exiting the car, Lee stabbed me in the left shoulder. Before he could pull it out, the police officer tackled him to the ground. Your dad grabbed a hold of me and held me for a few seconds, and then asked where you were. I didn't know where to tell him to look for you. I knew you were somewhere in an old barn fairly close, but Lee had me blindfolded most of the time. They rushed me to the hospital before I could see him again. He spent the last two days combing every inch of that old barn looking for you. They had a hidden door in the floor of the barn."

"Will you and my dad be okay?"

"I'll heal soon, and your dad will be okay now that you're alright."

"No, Elizabeth. Are you two still getting married?"

It was obvious that she knew what I meant, but I think she was afraid to allow her mind to go to that place. Before she could answer, my dad walked back into the room. I had seen him devastated over mom leaving and then ecstatic to have Elizabeth in his life. I was determined not to leave that room without them giving me some kind of reassurance that their wedding was still on.

"Dad, what is going on with you and Elizabeth?"

"What do you mean, honey?"

"I'm not a child. I can see you two aren't acting normal. You know this wasn't her fault."

Tears welled up in Elizabeth's eyes, and my dad was captured by her stare.

"Eli, I'm very sorry. If anything would have happened to Ruthy, I wouldn't have forgiven myself."

I elbowed my dad in the rib and motioned for him to go comfort her. Compassion was washing over his rough exterior. He went to Elizabeth's side, and they hugged.

"I'm sorry, Eli."

"I know, Beth. I was petrified of losing Ruthy. I can't lose her. How can I risk her life for my happiness? I felt it was my fault for getting involved with you, knowing the Balaamites had decreed to stop our marriage."

I had to interject after that revelation. "What do you mean you knew about the Balaamites' decree? You've heard of the Balaamites?"

"Ruthy, we were all trying to protect you. We thought it was best to keep all of that a secret."

My suspicion was growing with each word he spoke. "Dad, who do you mean when you say, 'we were all...?' Did Dan know about the decree?"

"Honey, don't get upset. We all knew about the decree. I, Elizabeth, Dan, Rawdy, Sarah, and everyone at the gathering knew the Balaamites had sent out a decree. It was only meant to stop our wedding; no one thought it had anything to do with you."

"Does it have anything to do with me?"

Dad looked at Elizabeth and then answered, "No...no, absolutely not. I'm sure you were just in the wrong place at the wrong time."

I did not know if I believed him or not, but it was obvious that neither one of them were going to tell me any different. It suddenly hit me that I had not seen Dan all morning.

"Where's Dan?"

Dad answered, "Honey, he was here late last night when you first came in. He wanted to stay longer, but he was called away by the General Council of Gatherings."

"Oh...that's right. I seem to be having trouble keeping my days straight."

"Dan is what you might call a spokesman for our gathering. He reports the events that take place here with our group. It is very important that they be informed of the Balaamite's actions. I'm sorry, honey. I know you would want him here, but you must know he would rather be here too. He'll be back soon."

Elizabeth said, "The council wanted him to come the day they found me, but he refused until he knew you were alright."

That information made me feel better. I knew Dan well enough to know he would do anything to keep me safe, and the last thing he would want to do is leave me unless he absolutely had to.

"So, where does this leave the two of you? I'm still expecting a wedding."

Dad was the first to speak, saying, "Ruthy, I don't know. I can't risk..."

"Dad, you are not putting me at risk. You love Elizabeth, and she loves you. We deserve to be happy. I will not let you, or anyone else, stop that wedding. I deserve to be happy, Dad. And you marrying Elizabeth will make me happy."

Dad sat on the bed next to Elizabeth, holding her hand. He reached into his pocket and pulled out her engagement ring. He held it between his thumb and first finger, as if he was looking at it for the first time, then he slipped it onto her finger. He leaned over and gently kissed her on the lips and then said, "How about I get my two girls out of this place? We have a feast to go to."

We left the hospital and dropped Elizabeth off at her house to change clothes, and then we drove to our home. Rawdy and Sarah were waiting on our front porch, thrilled to see me. Rawdy ran to the car and carried me into the house. I assured him I could walk, but he would not listen. They refused to leave my side until I demanded that I needed to change clothes. Finally, some privacy.

It was not until that moment that the gravity of the last six days hit me. The wind was knocked out of me, and I could not stop crying. Elizabeth and I had been only moments from being killed. Chad's father, Lee, had tried to stab her to death, and I might have starved to death if Dan had not sought God's help, and if Dad had not found the hidden door. I laid myself down on the bed, curled up in a ball, and held my stuffed teddy. Time seemed to stop, and only that moment was real. In that moment I was all alone, or at least I thought I was.

A fine mist filled the room, and I heard a voice speak, "Ruth, my child, I was with you the entire time. Do not be afraid. I have a plan for your life, and in the near future I will reveal the steps you are to take. Fear not, for I will be with you always."

I must have fallen asleep because the next thing I knew, Sarah was knocking on my door, saying it was time to leave. I quickly grabbed some clothes and ran in the bathroom to get ready. I was out in the car in less than fifteen minutes, and we were on our way to the luncheon. I did not tell anyone about my last encounter. Things were strange enough.

Dad informed me that the elders of our gathering wanted to talk with Elizabeth and me before the meal. We went to the large meeting hall that had once been a hospital. It was where we met every Sunday. There was a large room in the center of the building encircled with old concrete pillars. We entered the large room and saw a line of seven men sitting in ridiculously large, leather chairs. The chairs were ostentatious, but they did seem to fit the building's décor.

Mr. Tinker was an average size man in his early seventies. He officiated the meeting, starting with a formal request of God. He asked God to give them wisdom and direction in our situation. Then Mr. Tinker proceeded by recounting the prophetic word that had been given to Carl Gilpin.

Mr. Tinker said, "We have all heard of the Gilpin child that will be anointed in order to bring the town back to the knowledge of Jesus and the Truth. This child will be courageous, determined, bold, and full of faith and Godly wisdom."

He continued explaining how wonderful the child will be, but my mind was stuck contemplating my chances of being the "anointed child." It did not seem too likely to me. I said to myself, "Shy...check. Sheepish...check. I can be determined in certain situations. I'm not sure about being full of faith, but Godly wisdom. Me? I don't think so."

Mr. Tinker said, "Elijah and Elizabeth, because you are determined to proceed with your wedding plans, we are convinced the Balaamites will strike again."

A tall, slender man in his early fifties, Mr. Kinder, said, "And when the two of you decide to have children, we will take the appropriate precautions for your child's sake. Will you promise to let us know the minute you know you are expecting, Elizabeth?"

"Of course I will, sir."

Dad grabbed Elizabeth's hand.

Mr. Tinker questioned saying, "Are you sure we don't need to take precautions now for Ruth's sake?"

Mr. Kinder said, "What are you saying, Jeffery? Are you suggesting that Ruthy could be the anointed child?"

"Possibly. In the end, it's not what I believe that matters, but what the Balaamites believe that must dictate our actions. Do you deny that she was taken with Elizabeth and left to die?"

"No, but she might have just been an innocent eyewitness."

"Mr. Kinder, do you deny that miraculous events follow this girl?"

"No, but there have been others that have also experienced wondrous events such as young Daniel and Sarah. Even Eli has been miraculously healed and stands before us alive and healthy..."

Mr. Tinker stood up and said, "Enough! We all need to be on guard for anything that might happen to Elijah, Elizabeth, or Ruth. It is our responsibility as the leaders of this gathering to protect them." He looked straight at me and said, "Ruth?"

My mouth was dry, and I worked to get some saliva juices flowing so I could speak. "Yes, sir."

"Please step forward if you would."

I took a few steps.

"What is that necklace you are wearing?"

"My grandmother gave it to me."

"May I see it?"

I slipped the chain off over my head and placed it in Mr. Tinker's hand.

"The Guardian Thistle."

"Yes, sir."

"Which grandmother gave you this?"

"My dad's mother gave it to me."

Mr. Tinker looked up at my dad and asked, "Eli, are you familiar with the Findlays from Gilpinton?"

Dad replied, "I met Mr. Findlay at the Pumpkin Fest in October, but that is the extent of our acquaintance. Why do you ask?"

"It's probably nothing. I could swear I've seen this necklace before."

He handed the necklace back to me, and I slipped it back on.

"Ruth, you must give us your word that you will keep all of these events a secret."

Dad let go of Elizabeth's hand and took a step forward saying, "Mr. Tinker, how can you ask this of my daughter? The entire town knows she has been missing. Don't make her lie."

"Elijah, we would never think of asking her to...lie. Just omit the parts about the Balaamites and any miraculous events that she has experienced while here in Gilpinton."

Dad responded by saying, "Mr. Tinker, does the General Council agree with this? Wouldn't this miracle be a great tool to share with non-believers? It could help them know Jesus and the truth of salvation."

Mr. Kinder replied, "The council knows. This is their recommendation. You of all people, Eli, know where they stand on this issue. They haven't changed their position."

I was confused. Why would Dad know the council's position on this subject?

Dad tried to continue, saying, "But . . ."

Mr. Kinder took a step closer and said, "That is enough. We have spoken and that is final. Young Daniel will go to the General Council and explain our position. I do have one last request. We would like Mr. and Mrs. Clark to start meeting with Ruth on a weekly basis. You've already been meeting with him for pre-marriage counseling as a family, but we feel Ruth would greatly benefit from personal instruction from both Mr. Clark and his wife."

Mr. Kinder interjected, "Is this alright with you, Eli?"

Dad responded saying, "I trust Mr. and Mrs. Clark and agree it would be good for Ruthy, but for how long?"

"Three or four months should suffice. The Clarks have already agreed and will schedule with you at your next session."

Mr. Kinder turned his attention to me and asked, "Ruthy, do you have any questions?"

"Well, I was wondering if I've done something wrong."

"Of course not, dear."

"Then why do I need to meet with the Clarks?"

Mr. Tinker was the first to respond saying, "Ruth, you are a new believer who has experienced many miraculous and scary events. Normally, someone in your position would be taught the Word of God before anything of this magnitude would occur."

Mr. Kinder peered over at Mr. Tinker and said, "Usually it never does."

Mr. Tinker continued speaking. "We need to instruct you on the rules."

"There are rules?"

"Yes. If you go around telling everyone that people are being raised from the dead, they will start to believe you, and then what would happen?"

"More people will believe in Jesus."

"No. People will try to raise others from the dead, and when it doesn't work they will get mad at us."

"Why wouldn't it work, sir? It's what the words from God speak of, such as Lazarus and even Jesus."

"God reserved these things for special people."

"Special people like who?"

"The disciples and the prophets of old."

"I'm neither one of those, and yet you say some of these miracles happened because of me. How?"

Mr. Kinder said, "We're not sure. It doesn't make sense."

Mr. Tinker said, "We don't want other people getting their hopes up only to have them disappointed. It's not good for their faith."

Mr. Kinder walked over to my side and put his hand on my shoulder saying, "Ruthy, you are...how should I say? You're special. No, maybe unique would be a better description. Actually, you are extraordinary."

"I understand. I'm a freak."

Dad threw his arms around me trying to comfort and protect me with his embrace, but if I ever doubted I was a freak, the elders just proved it. There was something wrong with me, and they were going to try to fix me.

Mr. Tinker said, "Well, I think we all see why Ruth needs to meet with the Clarks."

In that moment, I felt stupid and ashamed, but why? What did I do to make these things occur? Why me? As if he knew my thoughts, Dad kissed my forehead and whispered, "It'll be alright. Don't worry. You're not in trouble." But that is exactly what I felt–for some reason, I was in trouble. Every miraculous event I experienced was similar to something in the words from God, and I was not even involved with Dan's death or bringing him back to life. All I had ever done was ask God to help me. How is that wrong? How could they think that was wrong?

The meeting lasted nearly two hours, and I was about to wet my pants. As soon as it ended, I rushed to the ladies' room. In the short time I was gone, the entire crowd had vacated the hall. The hall was completely empty, and yet it was starting to close in on me. I was alone.

I decided to go find my family. I started to walk out into the hall when I heard a man speaking. I was positive I heard my name. I could not help myself from eavesdropping on the conversation, so I slid around the corner, trying not to make a sound until I found the perfect position. I recognized the voice as that of Mr. Tinker. He was talking about Elizabeth and the prophesied child. I was unable to hear every word, but as I had suspected in the meeting, the man was half deaf, and even though it was obvious that he was trying to keep quiet, he was speaking loud enough that I had no trouble hearing him.

I heard another man say, "Are you sure she's the one?"

Then Mr. Tinker responded, "I am positive that Ruth is the promised child."

Those were the final words of their conversation. They both exited the hallway, assembling with the others in the dining room. I sank back against the cold concrete wall. I was distressed by Mr. Tinker's idea, but I did not have much time to process his words before Dad came looking for me.

"Come on, honey, you need to sit down and eat something. I know this has been a long ordeal, but it's over. We're all safe and sound."

It was reassuring to hear my dad's voice, even though it sounded like he was telling me that the big bad wolf was not going to hurt me anymore–it was something you would tell your five year old, not your teenager. I looked up at him and smiled. He put his arm around me, and I laid my head against his chest. I wished it had been a fairy tale that had frightened me, but I was not Little Red Riding Hood, and my wolf was not as easy to slay. My thoughts trailed off onto Dan, my hunter. It had only been a few hours since we had last spoken, yet my heart was yearning to be near him again. The idea of him being gone for any length of time seemed unbearable. I buried my head further into my dad's chest, looking for a place of comfort.

Dad ushered me into the dining room, grabbing me a plate full of food on our way to the table. What did Mr. Tinker mean? Was he really talking about me? How could I be the anointed child when I was not a blood relative, nor did I possess the Gilpin last name? I did not feel comfortable asking Elizabeth or my dad–I knew I would get in trouble for eavesdropping on the conversation, and Dan would not be calling for another couple of days. It had been a long day, and I decided to file the information away for another day, preferably a day when my life was not in danger.

The room was extremely quiet. Everyone was concentrating on their plate of food, eating instead of talking–those meals always have the best food. The room was filled with an air of peace–we were all safe and alive, at least for now. I gazed around the room and studied their faces–they all had the same expression. Satisfaction. They were the faces of the search party, my comrades...my friends...my family.

The Balaamites were still out there, and their threat was still real. None of us knew what our future held, but we knew we would face it together.

Epilogue – Temptation

DANIEL

"Boy, you will never catch me!" the scary, dark figure said.

I had been running for two miles and was completely out of breath–making it hard, but not impossible to say, "I'll get you if it's the last thing I do." But he was too fast for me and got away. I knew I had to get back to Naomi–no, I mean Ruthy–before the scary figure found her.

I started running for her house, but right before I reached her door, the house turned into the school. Why was I at the school? How did I get here? I opened the door and walked down the long hall. There standing at the end of the hall was Naomi–I do mean Naomi–my former love. It was as if some force was drawing me to her. I started walking toward her. Suddenly, she morphed into Ruthy. I stopped dead in my tracks. What is going on? I was positive I had seen Naomi, but that is impossible. I do not even think she lives in America. Just then Ruthy started saying, "Why are you doing this to me, Dan? Don't you care about me?"

I took a few steps closer and said, "Of course I care about you– I'm here to save you. He won't hurt you again." I started running toward her, but before I could touch her she was gone.

"Dan. Dan, where are you?" Naomi said. At the end of the long main hallway was another hallway that stretched to the right and to the left. I turned to my right and looked down the hallway.

Naomi was standing there with her arms extended. "Come to me, Dan. I still love you." I started walking toward Naomi.

Just then I heard Ruthy pleading with me saying, "Dan! Dan! Why are you doing this to me? Why are you hurting me, Dan?" I turned to my left and looked down the hallway. Ruthy was standing there crying.

I kept looking back and forth from my left then to my right. Why am I having a hard time choosing? How can this really be happening? Naomi is gone. Ruthy is here. Ruthy cares about me, and I care about Ruthy. Of course, I must go to her. I started running toward Ruthy, and half-way there she disappeared. She just vaporized. My mind must be playing games on me. I rubbed my eyes, trying to bring them into focus. Maybe I have an eye problem! Ruthy still was not there. With Ruthy gone, I turned around and ran toward Naomi. I stopped right before I got to her, and she started to say, "Dan, *Beep. Beep. Beep. Beep.*" This did not make any sense. What was she trying to say? Slowly the vision faded away as my alarm clock drew me from my dream. I leaned over and hit the snooze button.

"Dan? Dan, honey, it's time to get up." Mom was standing outside my door beckoning me to awaken. "Dan, are you awake? You need to be packed and out of here in an hour."

"I'm awake, Mom." I rolled out of bed and started to get dressed.

Mom was obviously up to something when she asked, "Can I come in and talk with you?"

"Yeah, come on in." I reached into my closet, pulling out my Jeep duffle bag and started to pack.

"Honey, do you really think you have gotten enough sleep to make this trip?"

"Yeah, I'm tired now, but I'll be fine."

"Well, I could call Mr. Clark for you and see if it would be okay for you to postpone a day or two."

"I promised Eli I would go in place of Ruthy and Elizabeth. I can't go back on my word. What would he think of me, Mom?"

"He would understand. I'm not telling you not to go. I just think it would be perfectly fine if you wait a day...maybe two. I want you to get some rest. I don't want to see you run down."

"Are you sure it would be okay for me to wait?"

"Oh, yes, honey! They will understand."

"I don't know."

"Please, let me make some calls and get it all set for you."

"Well, I would feel better if I could see Ruthy again, and maybe I could find out the decision from the meeting today. That way, I would have more to report to the council."

Mom was right. The council would allow me to get some rest. Ruthy and Elizabeth would be talking to our Board of Elders today, so I could be briefed on the elders' decision before I left for the council meeting. I could use some more sleep, and I would love to see Ruthy again. I had only been able to spend a few minutes with her in the hospital. It hardly felt real. I decided to take Mom up on the offer.

"That sounds like a great idea, Danny."

"Mom, please. I'm not a little boy anymore."

Mom came over to me and kissed me on the check saying, "You'll always be my little boy."

I gave her a hug and started to yawn.

"Okay, young *man*, get back into bed and sleep."

"Mom, would you make sure I'm awake in time to see Ruthy after the meeting?"

"Sure, honey. Now get back into bed." Mom walked around my bed and closed my shades, then she shut the door, but not before she said, "I'm so proud of you, Daniel."

I knew Mom was proud of me. This was what she had always dreamed for my life. Sure, she had spazzed out on me when I told her about being killed by a baseball bat, but what parent would not? She could not deny that God was working in my life and using me, and that had always been her request to God. She always asked God to use her four children for His purpose and to bring glory to His name. It was nice to hear her say she was proud of me. She had not been so excited about Ruthy and I being involved in any shape or form–nothing personally wrong with Ruthy. Although, Mom might think her family is questionable. But it had more to do with Mom's desire to see me become a gathering leader. She did not want me distracted.

My eyes were heavy, and before I knew it, my mom was waking me up again.

"Honey, it's time to get up. I've got food on the table. Dan, are you awake?"

"Yeah, Mom, I'll be right there."

I ate lunch, or was it breakfast? Well, it was actually both meals. I had enough time to take a shower and then get down to the gathering hall. I could hardly wait to see Naomi...oops, I mean Ruthy. Uggh, I have to stop that. *I care about Ruthy.* Naomi left me. I have to move on. That dream stirred up so many emotions. I had not even thought about Naomi in over a year. Well, at least not since Ruthy came to Gilpinton.

I drove my car to the hall, arriving just in time to see Ruthy and her family leaving. I jumped out and ran to her. She was standing in the doorway with her back to the street. Man, she is gorgeous and she does not even know it. The sunlight was glistening off of her highlights–she looked like a heavenly being radiating light.

I was able to surprise her, putting my hands over her eyes saying, "Guess who?"

"Dan!" Ruthy swung around, grabbing me around the neck, giving me a big hug. "I've missed you."

"Hi, Ruthy. I've missed you too." I could not get the ridiculous smile off of my face. I enjoyed seeing her smile and her beautiful eyes.

"I thought you'd left for the council meeting."

"Mom was able to persuade them to let me wait a day. She thought I needed to get some more rest."

"I'm so glad. So, you have to leave tomorrow?"

"Yeah."

She started to frown, and it was breaking my heart.

"Hey, I'm here now." I looked at Eli and asked, "Sir, may I give Ruthy a ride home?"

He looked at Elizabeth and then back at us. He had a smile on his face and said, "Sure. I think you've earned that privilege."

"Come on, Ruthy. I'm parked over here."

Now that I was here with her, I did not want to let her go. She had reluctantly stopped hugging me, and I knew she needed me to hold her hand. Ruthy had an incredibly hard year with her mom's leaving, that kid who killed himself, and her father finding someone to love again. I discovered if I made physical contact of some kind with her, such as holding her hand, she was able to relax and find normalcy. I knew after the week's ordeal that she needed to be comforted. She had no idea what God's plan was for her life, nor did she know who the elders and council believe she was or will become. In many ways she was like a baby, and I had to keep reminding myself of that fact. I had always been a believer, but she was so new to all of it.

I opened the car door, and she slid into the car. As I walked to my side, I knew my dream had been my heart's way of telling me that I had to come clean with Ruthy.

"Dan, it is so amazing to see you. I was disappointed when you weren't there this morning. I had resigned myself to the fact that I wouldn't see you again for a week or two. It's so good you're here."

She slid her left arm around my right one. She always thought too highly of me, and now I was going to let her down–just like everyone else.

"Ruthy, we need to talk."

"Sure! About what?"

"I need to tell you something." I was trying not to sound too serious.

"Is everything alright? Are you okay?"

"Yeah, as far as I know. I just need to explain something."

"Okay, shoot."

I wanted to be able to see her reaction, so I pulled the car over.

"Why did we stop here? I just live about a dozen houses from here." Concern was creeping its way across her face. I hate seeing her like that. I felt so responsible for her. It really was not that big of a deal. Just do it.

"I know you would like me to tell you that I love you, but I can't."

Shock filled her face as she said, "You don't love me?"

"That's not what I mean. It's not that I don't love you; it's that I can't say it. I can't...won't say that I love you until I know I can commit to marriage, and that is not possible for me right now.

"You've already told me this before. Why are you bringing this up now?" Aggravation was in her tone of voice.

"I had a dream about you last night."

A smile swept across her face. "Aw...you did?"

"But you weren't the only one in the dream with me."

"I wasn't?"

"No."

"So who was it?"

"Her name..." Ruthy interrupted me before I could get her name out.

"Her name? It was another girl?"

"Yes, Naomi is her name."

"Naomi! And who is Naomi?"

"Please, Ruthy, let me finish."

She folded her arms and gave me that look of disgust. "Go right ahead. I'm all ears."

"Naomi and I grew up together. Her mother and father were leadership of Gilpinton Community Gathering. She's a year older than I am, but that never seemed to matter–we've always been close friends. I think on some level I always liked her, but when she turned sixteen her parents gave a big party. It was very formal, and I had to wear a suit. Her parents hired a ballroom dancing instructor to come and teach us a couple dances. Naomi came over to me and asked me to be her partner, and I was hooked. She smelled so good, and her teeth were completely straight and porcelain white."

"Sounds like you're buying a horse."

I knew it could not be easy for Ruthy, so I decided to limit my narrative descriptions.

"We started hanging out after the gatherings, and our parents even had each other's families over for dinner once a week. I was only fifteen, but I thought I knew everything. I had very strong feelings for her, and I didn't know what to do. I was not even sure she felt the same. Six months after her birthday, Mom told me that Naomi and her parents had been in a horrible accident. Naomi was in serious condition, but both of her parents were dead. I went to the hospital and spent most of every day by her side. She made a full recovery without any permanent physical damage, but she blamed herself for the accident. Naomi had a hard time going on with life without her parents. Her grandfather decided to send her and her younger brother to live with relatives in Scotland. As soon as I heard, I rushed to see her and told her I loved her. She reciprocated the sentiment, but was gone within twenty-four hours. We wrote to each other for a while, but that slowly ended. I haven't heard from her in over a year."

"So do you still love her?" Ruthy said with great compassion and empathy, but I knew she was concerned where that left her.

"I don't think so. But the point is, I regret saying it to her. I always wanted the woman I told 'I love you' to be the one I married. I blew that already."

"So, where does that leave us?"

"Ruthy, I care about you deeply—more than I'll let myself express, but I can't offer you marriage for several years, and I don't want to make the same mistake twice."

"So, where does that leave us?" She repeated gingerly.

"I hope it leaves us right where we were. I felt you deserved an explanation, and after that dream of mine, I had to say something."

"What was the dream about?"

"Well, we were all three at the school, and down one hall you were standing, and down another Naomi was standing. Naomi kept calling me to her, and you kept asking me why I was hurting you."

"I would never think that about you. You saved my life."

"I know, but I think it was my heart telling me I have to be totally honest with you and tell you about Naomi."

"You still care about me, right?"

"Yes, of course I do."

"Well, then I'm satisfied. And this girl is in another country, so there is no need for you to worry about this again." Ruthy leaned across the car and gave me a hug. "Dad will be home by now, so we better get going."

I started up the car and headed for her house. After a short moment of silence, Ruthy said, "Thanks for being honest with me. That is something rare in my life. Promise me you will always be honest with me, even if it might hurt my feelings."

"I hope I never have to keep that promise, but of course, I promise to always be honest with you."

I drove up into her driveway, expecting her to say goodbye, but Eli was standing in the driveway motioning us to come inside. "Dan, I have those salmon steaks thawed, and there's a game on tonight. Would you like to come in?"

"Sure, sir. I would love to if it's okay with you, Ruthy." I was concerned that my latest revelation had thrown her for a loop. She looked at me for a minute then replied, "Of course it's fine with me. I always love it when you're here."

Eli went into the house and started cooking with Elizabeth while Ruthy and I sat on the porch swing. "Dan, I know life can be crazy, and we never know exactly how or when the twists and turns will come, but I want you to know that it meant a lot to me that you would share about Naomi. I trust you."

The meal was superb as usual. We all settled into the living room when the door bell rang. Eli got up and went to answer the door. "Rawdy...Sarah...it's great to see you guys. Come on in."

Rawdy and Sarah found their seats and settled in for the game. I looked around the room, trying not to be obvious. It felt good to be in this group. Ruthy caught my eye and smiled. I think she was making the same assessment of the crowd. It all seemed so right...so perfect. I could hardly wait to make this a permanent event. Just then, Sarah interrupted my thoughts saying, "Hey, Dan, guess who we just saw down at the QT?"

"Who was it?" I am never good at those guessing games, and Sarah knows it too.

"It was Naomi. She said that she and Bo moved back to Gilpinton today."